James Grant

Scots Brigade

James Grant

Scots Brigade

ISBN/EAN: 9783337332020

Printed in Europe, USA, Canada, Australia, Japan

Cover: Foto ©Andreas Hilbeck / pixelio.de

More available books at **www.hansebooks.com**

THE
SCOTS BRIGADE'

AND OTHER TALES

BY

JAMES GRANT
AUTHOR OF 'THE ROMANCE OF WAR'

' The dying and dead strewed the breach at Meenen,
Where our brave Scottish blades met the troops of Turenne ;
When cannon and firelock and musketoon played,
As often, elsewhere, on the old Scots Brigade !
Holland's Bulwark—in many a battle of yore—
From the woods of Brabant to the far Frisian shore ;
Never Frenchman, nor Spaniard, nor German essayed
To withstand the hot charge of the old Scots Brigade !'
Camp Song.

LONDON
GEORGE ROUTLEDGE AND SONS
BROADWAY, LUDGATE HILL
NEW YORK: 9, LAFAYETTE PLACE
1882

CONTENTS.

———◦✕◦———

THE SCOTS BRIGADE :

THE SCOTS BRIGADE.

THE SCOTS BRIGADE.

CHAPTER I.

THE LOVER.

'AND you will not accompany me to call on these ladies, uncle ?' said the young man persuasively.

'Certainly not, boy; do you take me for a fool—der Duyvel!' was the snappish rejoinder, as the General tossed his silver-mounted meerschaum on the table. and thrust his chair back on the polished oak floor, 'I have suspected you for some time past, and know, from old experience, that a young fellow in love is lost to the service and himself; among women he is as helpless as a rudderless ship among the thousand shoals of the Zuyder Zee! You are my heir, as you know, provided your conduct and obedience satisfy me. I am rich enough for both of us, and I had begun to hope that, like me, you would go through the world without the encumbrance of a wife. I shall not see you make a fool of yourself, without making an effort to save you. I shall give you a Beating Order, and send you to recruit for the Brigade in Scotland ; or how would you like to roast on detachment at Guayana, or among the Dutch Isles in the Caribbean Sea ?'

'Such a separation would be death to me, and to Dolores too.'

'Dol—what ?' roared the General, grasping the knobs of his arm-chair and glaring at the speaker; 'how familiar we are, it seems ! Where the devil did she get that absurd name ?'

'From a Spanish ancestress, and with the name much of her beauty,' replied the younger man, who had a very pleasant voice and manner, which, if somewhat sad and soft, possessed the charm of cultured influences and refinement.

'Dolores—a very Donna Dulcinea, no doubt ! Well, my young cock-o'-the-game, it is useless in me to repeat what you don't want to hear, and in you to say the same thing over and over again, as you have been doing for the last hour. So far as you and this —Dolores are concerned, my mind is made up—yes, by the henckers' horns !'

The speaker was no Dutchman, as his interjection

might lead the reader to infer, but, like his nephew, a native of the northern portion of our isle, being Lieutenant-General John Kinloch, of Thominean in Fifeshire, Colonel-Commandant of the six battalions of the Scots Brigade, in the service of their High Mightinesses the States-General of Holland—a corps which boasted itself 'the Bulwark of the Republic'— a veteran of more than twenty years' hard service, though still in the flower of manhood.

His hair was powdered and queued, as was then the fashion ; his handsome face was well bronzed by long exposure to the tropical sun, and his hands, which had never known gloves, contrasted in their brown hue with snow-white ruffles of the finest lace at the wide cuffs of his uniform coat.

His nose was straight; his mouth expressed firmness and decision, and his dark eyes, which were sparkling then with no small amount of anger, had somewhat shaggy brows that nearly met in one, and gave great character to his face.

His nephew, who stood near him, playing with the gold knot of his sword, and trying to deprecate his anger, was Lewis (or as he was generally called Lewie) Baronald of that Ilk in Lanarkshire (the only son of a baronet attainted after Culloden), and now a handsome young lieutenant in the Earl of Drumlanrig's Battalion of the Scots Brigade, in quarters, where we find him, at the Hague.

His face wore a droll expression just then, in spite of himself, as he knew that his uncle and patron was well known in the Brigade, and in Dutch society, as a misogynist—a genuine woman-hater, under the influence of some never-forgotten disappointment he had endured in early life, and who never omitted by the exertion of his advice, influence, or actual authority, to mar—if possible—the matrimonial views and wishes of the officers and men under his command.

When any of his brother officers would venture to express their surprise that one who was evidently so good-hearted and warm by nature, and who—though in all things a perfect soldier—was apparently fond of domestic life, should have omitted to share it with a help-mate, their remarks only invoked a torrent of grotesque invectives upon the sex, and put the General in such exceeding bad humour, that they were glad to beat a retreat and leave him to himself.

He had begun to perceive that for some time past, his nephew was abstracted in manner, that he absented himself from his quarters, was rather estranged from his comrades, and was almost neglectful of his military duties; and from rumours that reached him from the idlers and promenaders in the Voorhout and on the Vyverberg, the General was not long in discovering that a charming young girl was the cause of all this, and great was his wrath thereat. And when he found that Lewie Baronald's abstraction increased ; that he caught him reading poetry instead of studying the ' *Tactique et Discipline de Prusse*' ; that he sighed sometimes involuntarily, and more than once had been caught inditing suspicious-looking little missives in the form of delicately folded, tinted and perfumed notes, he took him finally to task, and his indignation found vent, as it did on the present occasion.

' And you fell in with this girl——'

' When our battalion was sharing duty with the Dutch Guards at the Prince of Orange's palace in Amsterdam.'

' And how about her mother?' growled the General.

' She was very averse to my attendance on her daughter till——'

' Till when or what?' snapped the uncle.

' She asked me some questions concerning my name and family, and then suddenly I became quite a favourite.'

' All cunning—all cunning ! But our name and our blood are as good as any in Holland, and better than some, I suppose ; but every Scot has a pedigree, as King James was wont to say.'

And as General Kinloch spoke, the strong old

Scottish accent, which then prevailed at the Bar and in the Pulpit at home (as it had done at Court in the preceding century), deepened with his excitement and irritation.

'And the mother is a widow, Drumlanrig tells me,' he continued ; 'a widow who, I doubt not, loves her coffee with a glass of good curaçoa from De Pylsteeg at Amsterdam.'

'Indeed you mistake her, uncle,' replied the young man indignantly.

'Umph—egad—do I ?'

'She often speaks to me of you, uncle.'

'Does she ? I am greatly honoured.'

'Yes—and seems to know all about you, and your brilliant services to their Mightinesses the States, and so forth.'

'The devil she does ! Well, she probably knows also that I never was a lady's man—a lady-killer, a buck, or a blood in my time ; so my lady countess may spare her breath to cool her porridge. And *who* is this Countess van Renslaer ? Her name sounds new to me.'

'She has but lately come to Holland.'

'From where ?'

'England last, I believe ; and none seem to take a higher place at the Court of the Prince of Orange, at the balls of the Grand Pensionary, and of the richest burgers in the Hague and Amsterdam.'

'Ouf! Well, I go to none of them—not even to Court, save once a year, to kiss the Prince's hand, and give in the Brigade Reports. She has a great retinue —keeps a stately coach and two sedans, I hear; and does this artful old — countess seem to tolerate the advances of a penniless sub like you, to her daughter?'

'Yes.'

'Why?'

'Because she is interested in me,' replied Lewie Baronald, smiling.

'For what reason?'

'Her first lover had been one of the Scots Brigade, and her heart still warms to the uniform.'

The knitted brow of the General relaxed for a moment, and he said with a grim smile:

'Then there have been two fools at least in the Brigade, to my knowledge. And for this prize, Dolores—I have caught her absurd name, you perceive—have you no rivals—no competitors?'

The young man's brow grew very dark.

'Yes,' said he, after a pause.

'Many?'

'One chiefly.'

' Whom you fear ?'

' I fear no man that wears a sword, uncle! She has a cousin, called Maurice Morganstjern, whom I greatly distrust.'

' Grandson of that Morganstjern who was one of the assassins of the De Witts in the last century? Avoid the whole brood, I say! If you will not be guided by me, who have your interest at heart, consult your Colonel, Drumlanrig, on this matter, and hear what *he* will say.'

' The last man to consult on such a topic.'

' Why ?'

' Like yourself, he shuns female society. He is a gloomy misanthrope, and one of a fated race.'

' Right : a curse fell on his house, for the duke's share in the Union of 1707. I thought your family troubles were at an end when you joined the Brigade ; but, der Duyvel! they seem only beginning, with this Dolores. To me it appears that there are some families—in Scotland more especially—whom misfortune—fate—which you will—pursueth to utter destruction.'

' The fate of mine was their own choosing : it lay between prudence and loyalty, and ill would it have become my people to have wavered when the Royal Standard was unfurled in Glenfinnan.'

'Your father's views and mine were different in that matter,' said the General in a softer tone.

'Give me your hand. I do not despair of your favour for us yet.'

'Indeed!'

'Tyne heart, tyne all, as we say at home.'

'In old Scotland, yes—and before the enemy, that is well enough ; but anent a woman—go—go—or I shall lose my temper again. Besides, Lewie, there is a cloud on the horizon—the political horizon, I mean —which, though as yet no bigger than a man's hand, may expand into a dark and mighty one of storm and bloodshed. A revolution is at hand in France, and a time is coming when we—the Scots Brigade— will have other work than love-making cut out for us, and we shall have to choose between casting our lot forever with the States-General or with his Majesty George III.; for there is not a tavern and not a caserne in Holland in which the matter is not debated keenly and hotly now.'

Though the steady opposition and hostility of his uncle and patron, on whom all his hopes depended, left the young man depressed in spirit and heavy in heart, and inspired by no small dread of separation from the object of his love, he quitted the General's house, and set forth to visit her.

2

CHAPTER II.

THE COLONEL-COMMANDANT.

THE General refilled his glass and his meerschaum, and remained sunk in thought after the departure of his nephew, and more than once he sighed heavily, knit his brows, and shook his head.

He was not drinking schiedam with water, but good Farintosh whisky, kegs of which were regularly sent to him by a Scottish merchant from the Scotsch Dyk at Rotterdam—Farintosh which was then free from all Excise duty, and remained so till five years after the period of our story.

We have said that General Kinloch was a handsome man and in the flower of manhood ; and a fine picture he would have made as he sat there, in his graceful old-fashioned uniform, with heavily-laced lapels and skirts, his hair powdered and queued, with a Khevenhüller hat (not unlike that of Napoleon I.) close by, adorned with a stiff upright feather and Dutch cockade, and his silk sash worn crossways in the old Scottish fashion.

The old Scottish officer who took a turn of service in France was jaunty in air, tone, and bearing, as

Scott describes his Baron of Bradwardin to have been ; but his countryman who served the States of Holland became, under the influence of his flat, stale and stolid surroundings, rather another style of man —equally brave and gallant in war, but less gallant in the ball-room or the boudoir—often grave, grim, and starched amid the influence of Dutch society and Presbyterianism.

It was only thirty-four years before that Culloden had been fought ; and though his political sympathies were not with the exiled King James VIII., his mind was full of the bitter memories of that atrocious field left in every right-thinking Scottish heart ; and his orphan nephew, Lewie Baronald, was the son of his only sister, one of those enthusiastic Jacobite ladies who kept guard at Edinburgh Cross with a drawn sword when the King was proclaimed, who danced at the famous Holyrood ball, and who, like more than one old lady in Scottish history and tradition, had never allowed her husband to kiss her, after the Prince did so, and after making his bed, when an exile and fugitive, with her own hands, had laid aside the sheets thereof to be a shroud for herself, in the true spirit of loyalty 'and that sublime devotion which the Saxon never knew.'

Long as he had been in Holland, the eyes of our

Scot—accustomed as he had been to the grand mountain scenery of his native land—had never become
accustomed to the utter monotony, flatness, and in-
sipidity of the Dutch landscape, or to the brusqueness
of the natives, their stolidity and general dulness of
demeanour ; but the pay was good, the quarters were
comfortable, and—when not fighting—the service was
easy enough. His sword was almost his inheritance,
as the estate he inherited, Thominean, was drowned
in debt ; and their High Mightinesses the States-
General were sure and generous paymasters.

Yet, times there were when he thought with the
author of ' Vathek,' that there must have been a period
when Holland was all water, ' and the ancestors of
the present inhabitants fish. A certain *oysterishness*
of eye and flabbiness of complexion are almost proof-
sufficient of this aquatic descent ; and pray tell me for
what purpose are such galligaskins as the Dutch burthen
themselves with contrived, but to tuck up a flouncing
tail, and thus cloak the deformity of a dolphin-like
termination.'

Reflecting angrily and sadly upon the recent conversation with his favourite, the General continued to
smoke and gaze down the long vista of the quaint
Dutch street, with its stiff rows of trees reflected
downward in the canal that lay parallel with them,

and its quaint gables on each of which, nearly, a stork was perched ; the little mirrors projecting from the windows to enable the ladies within to see those who passed outside ; the knockers tied up with pincushions and plaited lace to indicate that a 'goodwife was in the straw.'

There were women in the mobcaps, print-gowns, and gaudy satin aprons worn by all ranks alike ; men in broad, round, conical hats, puckered jackets, and ca‧ pacious breeches, now no longer to be seen but in very remote districts ; an occasional dominie or clergyman in his court-like costume, ruff and cocked hat, passing homeward after having a pipe with some parishioner, or a dish of coffee with his vrouw.

There was the clatter of wooden shoes in the ill-paved street ; the oil-lamps were beginning to glimmer like glow-worms, and were reflected in the slime of the canals ; the drums and fifes of the Scots Brigade, in the adjacent caserne, were playing out the dying day, and sweetly stole upon the ambient evening the old air :

> 'Oh, the Lowlands o' Holland
> Hae parted my love and me ;'

but the General was in shadow-land, thinking of other times and long-vanished faces, and wondering when the guilders of their High Mightinesses, and the prize‧

money won from the French and Spaniards, would free his inheritance from all its wadsets and incumbrances, and he would be able to hang his sword, where still his father's hung, in the old dining-hall of Thominean.

He saw it in fancy, that old house of Thominean ('the hill of birds'), with its grey crow-stepped gables and conical pepper-box turrets of the days of James VI., overlooked by the green range of the lovely Ochills; and he laughed softly as he remembered how in boyhood there he had trembled at the thought of the tiny elves, who, on their festival nights, were alleged to make great noises under the green turf, opening and shutting large chests of gold, and clattering with goblets and copper kettles; and how still more did he tremble at the story of a mysterious mirror, in which occasionally the figure of a pale woman, clad in white, could be distinctly seen *behind* the reflection of the person who stood before the glass, and how it was said to have appeared therein on the night his beloved sister, the Lady Baronald, died, and left her only son penniless in the world.

Thus Lewie, in his boyhood, became a soldier. On an evening that he never forgot, there came marching bravely down the quaint High Street of Kinross a recruiting-party of the Scots Brigade, with ribbons fluttering, drawn swords gleaming, the shrill pipes and hoarse drums, making every lane and alley bordering on Loch Leven to re-echo 'The Lowlands o' Holland ;' and halting in front of the Bruce Arms Inn, a portly sergeant, after a libation of Farintosh had been duly poured forth, harangued the gathered rustics. He invited ' all lads of spirit to join that battalion of the Scots Brigade, commanded by the noble and valiant Henry Douglas, Earl of Drumlanrig, under their High Mightinesses the States-General of Holland, to fight the frog-eating French and popish Spaniards; all who so entered to have complete new clothing, arms and accoutrements as became a gentleman and soldier, two guineas bounty, and a crown to drink to the health of their High Mightinesses, and to the confusion of their enemies !'

A loud hurrah and much brandishing of broadswords followed this invitation, and ere 'The Point of War' was fully beaten, Lewie Baronald had shaken hands with this Scottish Sergeant Kite, and had the Dutch cockade pinned on his blue bonnet by a cunning corporal, who showed him an old watch like a silver turnip, and worth half-a-crown, which he boldly alleged had been presented to him ' by his Royal Highness the Prince of Orange in person.'

His uncle's influence soon procured him 'a pair of

colours,' as the phrase was then, for a commission; and he soon proved himself worthy of the distinction by the daring and courage he displayed, when the battalion of Drumlanrig was employed with other Dutch troops in 1774, at the Cape of Good Hope, in driving the natives from the Bokkeveld and Roggeveld, back into the deserts on the south-west coast of Africa; and since his return to Holland his name, the popularity of his regiment, his handsome face and figure, were equally passports to the best society in the Hague and at Amsterdam.

But now, it seemed to his uncle and patron, the Colonel-Commandant of the Brigade, that his prospects were on the point of being marred by this unlucky passion for the daughter of the Countess van Renslaer.

Kinloch's antipathy to women was well known in the Brigade, and it was a standing joke among the battalions, that once, when the coquettish wife of the Grand Pensionary of Amsterdam had lured him into a game of battledore and shuttlecock, and contrived to let the latter drop into her ample bosom, and pointing thereto, piteously besought the General to take it out, that he—obtuse as Uncle Toby with the Widow Wadman—deftly abstracted it with the tongs.

'The lad will succeed me in time, as Laird of

Thominean,' he muttered, after a time; 'the forfeited baronetcy may be restored: so why shouldn't he marry because I—I—but better not! They are all alike—all alike, these women: so he will be safer with the left wing of Dundas's Battalion in the West Indies, than philandering here at the Hague.'

But even while giving utterance to his thoughts, his features relaxed: his irritation or annoyance seemed to abate as other thoughts stole into his mind, and a shade of melancholy came over his face; and resting his head upon his hands, he remained for a time in deep and apparently painful thought.

Then he rose slowly, and selecting a key from a small bunch, opened an elaborately-carved Dutch cabinet, and from a secret drawer thereof, curiously and ingeniously hidden by a movable lion's head, he drew forth the oval miniature of a young girl, and gazed upon it long, sorrowfully, and tenderly.

There was something quaint and childlike in the beauty of the girl depicted there, with a string of pearls round her white and slender throat. Her complexion was clear and pure, her expression innocent, with golden-brown hair, and golden-brown eyes that seemed to smile on him again as he gazed on them.

A hot tear started in the eyes of Kinloch, yet he bit his lip, and, as if angry with himself for the emotion that came over him, he closed the miniature-case with a sharp snap, and restored it to its place of concealment hurriedly, muttering :

'Fool that I was—fool that I am now ! Heaven grant that this Dolores of Lewie's may not make the dupe of him that girl made of me ! I must save him from himself. I shall write the Director-General of the Forces—Berbice or Essequibo it must be. Poor Lewie ! I am loth to part with him ; but, der Duyvel ! he shall not be the victim of this old jade and her daughter.'

CHAPTER III.

SWORD-PLAY.

FULL of conflicting thoughts Lewie Baronald, with a slower pace than usual, proceeded towards the residence of the Countess van Renslaer, and quitting the Lang Vourhout, he crossed the canal that encircles the whole Hague.

If compelled by his powerful uncle's eccentric opposition to act the laggard now, he might leave Dolores to be won by his rival Morganst-

jern ! Such things have been, and may be
again. His brain whirled and his heart sank at the
thought ; and even if he had the permission of the
Director-General of Infantry accorded him, could he
ask the brilliant Dolores to share his solitary room
in the barracks—the *Oranje Caserne*—of the Scots
Brigade ?

The thought was full of folly and presumption.
He was not quite aware of the full extent of the
hostile—yet well-meant—design his uncle the General
was forming, for an effectual separation between him
and the object of his love. He had left her yesterday
with the avowed intention of obtaining the sanction
of the General, from whom he had a yearly allowance :
and now that the sanction was withheld, he was in
sore perplexity, for by the then rules of the Dutch
service no officer could marry without the consent of
his superior ; and how was he to tell Dolores that
this had been bluntly refused, and that even exile or
foreign service menaced him ?

While these thoughts were passing through his
mind, he came suddenly upon Maurice Morganstjern ;
he was seated under one of the trees that bordered
the canal near the Hooge Wal, and was leisurely
polishing the blade of his rapier with his leather glove,
while conversing with a friend.

He was rather a handsome but dissipated-looking young fellow, and had shifty eyes and a very sinister expression of face. He wore his sandy-coloured hair powdered and tied, a smart Nivernois hat (such hats were all the rage about 1780), small, and with the flaps fastened up to the brim with hooks and eyes; his costume was bright in colours and richly laced.

That of his companion was the reverse. He wore an old battered Khevenhüller hat; his shaggy hair was unpowdered; his ruffles were soiled and torn; his visage was bloated and his eyes bloodshot and watery, while a scar on his nose, covered by a piece of black court-plaster, did not add to the respectability of his appearance: and Lewie Baronald, who knew him to be the Heer van Schrekhorn, a noted bully, gamester, and frequenter of gambling-houses and estaminets, barely accorded him any recognition, though feeling himself compelled to present his hand to Maurice Morganst-jern.

'How now, Mynheer—have you been fighting?' he inquired laughingly of the latter.

'No; only polishing some specks off my sword,' replied Morganstjern, with a smile on his thin lips, though there was none in his watery grey eyes; 'but apropos of fighting—do you affect that?'

'In a proper cause—yes,' replied Baronald, surprised by the question.

'And can cover yourself well?' continued Morganstjern, making a half-mock lunge which the other—
with the quickness of lightning—parried by his sword
which he instantly drew.

'I can cover myself, as you shall see,' he exclaimed;
and they began to fence in jest apparently, while the
Heer looked approvingly on, and said with a laugh
and an oath:

'Now we shall see who is the better ruffler of the two.'

And the Heer, who bore Lewie no goodwill for the
coldness of his demeanour and the general hauteur
he manifested towards him, looked as if he would
very much have relished to draw his old hanger and
engage in the perilous sport too—for perilous it was,
with keen-edged and sharply-pointed straight-bladed
swords.

The Heer van Schrekhorn was everyway an odious
fellow—a lover of the fair sex, of schiedam and cards;
but one who always avowed openly that *liking* for a
woman was one thing, but love for her was another—
and certes he knew nothing about it.

He loudly and bluntly applauded his friend's
fencing.

'Appel now!' he exclaimed; 'quick—disengage to

that side again! contract your arm—quick—dart a
thrust right forward now!'

At that moment, as if in obedience to the suggestion,
the point of Morganstjern's sword struck the gilded
regimental gorget of Baronald, which was adorned
with the Lion Rampant of the Netherlands.

'The devil!' he exclaimed; 'do you aim at my
throat?'

'All a mistake,' said Morganstjern, beginning to
pant as he was pressed on in turn and driven back.

'Is this folly or fury—do you really wish to quarrel?'
asked Lewie Baronald; but the other made no reply,
though his eyes became inflamed, his colour deepened,
his teeth were set and his brows knit; and though he
laughed, the sound of his laughter was strange and
unnatural.

This game at sharps was certainly jest with Baronald,
though he little liked his opponent; but he soon
became aware that the eyes of the latter seemed to
become more bloodshot, that his cheek paled, his
grasp grew firmer on his hilt; that his thrusts came
quickly and fiercely—in short, that beyond all doubt,
under cover of a little pretended sword-play, he had—
murder in his heart!

They were rivals for the love of Dolores, yet Morganstjern had not the courage to challenge Baronald

to a regular mortal duel. His bearing now, and the perilous thrust arrested by his gorget, were a warning to the latter of that which Morganstjern was now capable—killing him by design, without peril to himself, while he would affect that it was done by mere chance in rough jest ; and had Baronald been run through the body, the Heer would have been ready to affirm and swear that it was all done by the merest accident.

Baronald felt his blood getting warm ; he knew that duelling was sternly discouraged by the Dutch authorities ; and that to kill the cousin of Dolores, even in self-defence, would preclude all chance of possessing her favour.

But a strong measure was absolutely necessary. Darting forward he suddenly locked-in—seized his adversary's sword-arm, by twining his left arm round it, thus closing his parade hilt to hilt, and disarmed him by literally wrenching his sword from his grasp.

Pale as death now, panting, and with eyes flashing fire, Morganstjern stood before the victor, who, presenting the captured sword by the blade, said, with a kind of smile :

' This rough play is being carried too far—here let it end.'

Hissing out some execration, Morganstjern took his sword by the hilt, and in the blind excesss of his fury would have plunged it into the breast of Baronald, but at the moment it was struck up by another sword, as two officers of the Scots Brigade, Francis, Lord Lindores, and the Master of Dumbarton, threw themselves between them.

'We do but jest, gentlemen,' said Morganstjern, lifting his hat and sheathing his sword.

'Is this true, Baronald?' asked Lord Lindores.

'Jest assuredly, so far as I am concerned,' replied Lewie.

'I must confess that the work looked remarkably like earnest, so far as your adversary was concerned,' remarked the Master of Dumbarton, with a look at Morganstjern which there was no mistaking ; but the latter simply bowed, and saying :

'Gentlemen—your servant. I have the honour to bid you good evening.'

Then, accompanied by the Heer van Schrekhorn, he hastened away ; leaving Baronald to explain the matter as he chose to his two brother-officers, who had some difficulty in making him really aware of the deadly risk he had run.

'He is gone like a man who has lost an hour and runs as if to overtake it,' said Lord Lindores. 'Now how

came you, Lewie Baronald, to be fencing, even in
jest, with rufflers such as these?'

Baronald could not explain that one of them was
the cousin of Dolores.

'At the Kanongieterv we have just parted with
Van Otterbeck, the Minister of State. It is as well he
did not accompany us and see that piece of folly,
Baronald ; it might have gone hard with you, as the
Brigade is not greatly in favour just now,' said the
Master of Dumbarton, who was James Douglas,
grandson of the loyal and gallant Earl of that title,
who was Colonel of the Royal Scots, and followed
James VII. into exile.

He was tall, had a straight nose, the bold dark
eyes of the Douglas race, and sunny brown hair tied
behind with a black ribbon and rosette.

'True,' added Lord Lindores ; 'and I begin to
think the Brigade has had enough and to spare of
Holland during these two hundred years past, fighting
to defend lazy boors and greedy merchants, in a land
of frowsy fogs and muddy canals ; as Butler has it in
" Hudibras :"

> '" A land that rides at anchor, and is moored ;
> In which they do not live, but go aboard." '

These remarks referred to the growing discontent
between the regiments of the Brigade and the States-

General—matters to which we may have to refer elsewhere, and which led to the former abandoning the service of the latter for that of Great Britain.

And now Lewie Baronald, after thanking his friends for their intervention and advice, took the road to the residence of the Countess van Renslaer, whither, unknown to him, Morganstjern had preceded him, and was, at that very moment, engaged with Dolores.

CHAPTER IV.

DOLORES.

THE villa occupied by the Countess van Renslaer stood a little distance from the Hague, on the Ryswick road, amid a large pleasure-garden in the old Dutch style, a marvel of prettiness, with its meandering walks, fantastically-cut parterres, box borders, pyramids of flower-pots, and tiny fish-pond where the carp and perch were often fed by the white hands of Dolores.

It had more than one rose-bowered *zomerhuis* hidden among the shrubbery, and admirably adapted for contemplation or flirtation. It was the month of May now, when the tulips and hyacinths, potted in *jardinières* full of light sand, were in all their beauty—flowers for which, in the days of the *tulip-mania*, a hundred florins had been paid for a single bulb.

Around, the country was intersected in every direction by canals and trees in long straight avenues, the level surface dotted with farms and summer-houses ; an occasional steeple, the old castle where the famous Treaty of Ryswick was signed, and the sails of many windmills whirling slowly in the evening breeze, alone broke the flat monotony of the Dutch horizon.

In the deep recess of a window that opened to the garden sat Dolores, watching and expectant. But only that morning, after parade, Lewie Baronold had talked to her of love—his love and hers—in the recess of that window—talked so sweetly of his adoration of her own charming self. So Dolores had thought to sit there again, with eyes half closed and smiling lips, to think it all over once more, while fanning herself with one of the large fans of green silk then in fashion, while the Countess, her mother, had fallen asleep over 'Clélia,' one of Monsieur de Scudery's five-volume folio novels, in the drawing-room beyond.

Dolores was taller, more lithe and slender, than Dutch girls usually are, for she had in her veins the blood of more than one ancestor who had come with that scourge of the Low Countries, Ferdinand of

Toledo, *el castigador del Flamencas ;* hence her graceful figure, the stately carriage of her beautiful head,
her rather aquiline and oval features, her dark hair,
and the darker lashes that shaded her soft eyes that
were 'like violets bathed in dew,' and hence her
peculiar name of Dolores.

She had the bloom of Holland in her cheek, and the
grace of Spain in her carriage and bearing. An
exquisite costume of pale yellow silk became the
brunette character of her beauty well ; creamy lace
fell away in folds from the snowy arms it revealed ;
perfume, brilliance, and softness were about her.

There was a step on the gravel ; her colour
deepened.

'Morganstjern—Cousin Maurice !' she muttered with
a tone of annoyance, as he approached her with hat in
hand.

Would this creature, so incomparably lovely and
winning, ever belong to him, and lie in his bosom ? he
was thinking as he surveyed her ; was she not rather
drifting away from him, and would soon, unless he
took strong and sure measures with yonder accursed
Schottlander, be lost to him and his world for ever ?

'Always becomingly dressed, Dolores,' said he,
stooping over her ; 'but this costume especially suits
your style of loveliness.'

'You must not say such things to me,' she replied with some asperity.

'How—why?'

'I mean such pretty or complimentary things, Maurice Morganstjern ; because if you do——'

'What then ?'

'I shall think that I have forfeited your friendship.'

'Friendship !' said he gloomily ; 'how long will you seem to misunderstand me ?'

Try as she might, Dolores could not feel kindly or well disposed towards her cousin Morganstjern, and her replies to him always sounded cold and formal, or taunting even to herself; and the face that bent over her was, she knew, not a good one, but sinister, and expressive of a bad and evil spirit within.

And now, as a somewhat palpable hint that his conversation wearied or worried her, she took up her flageolet, and putting the ivory mouthpiece to her rosy lips, began to play a sweet little air, while his brow became darker, for this now obsolete instrument (which had silver stops like the old English flute) had been a gift of Lewie Baronald's, who, in the gallantry of the day, had inserted a copy of verses addressed to herself, and which, of course, would only be found when the instrument was unscrewed to discover what marred its use.

Anon she paused; Maurice Morganstjern then glanced towards the Countess, and perceiving that she still slept, drew nearer to Dolores, and lowering his voice, said :

'Can you not love me a little, cousin ?'

'Not as you wish,' she replied.

'Why ?'

The musical voice of Dolores broke into a soft little laugh as she fanned herself, and said :

'Simply because one cannot love two persons at once.'

'Meaning that you love this—this accursed Schottlander ?' he hissed through his set teeth.

'Oh, Maurice ! how can you be so rude as to speak thus of any visitor of mamma's !'

'Listen to me, Cousin Dolores,' he resumed, making a prodigious effort to be calm.

'Well,' asked the girl, with something of petulance.

'I am probably to be sent to Paris.'

'Indeed—for what purpose ?'

'In the interests of the patriots here.'

'And against the Prince of Orange ?'

'Yes—of course.'

'You are unwise to say this to me even, cousin,' said she, looking up now.

'But you, Dolores, are my second self.'

'What will you do when I go?'

'Much the same as I did before you honoured the Hague with your presence.'

'To me it seems that you care little whether you see me or not.'

'What then?—and it may be so. Cousin Maurice, you are always annoying me by love-making, or by scowling and taunting me about gentlemen visitors.'

'May I hope, however, that you will pay me the compliment of feeling my absence—of missing me a little?'

'That,' replied the provoking beauty, as an arch expression stole into her face, 'may depend upon what amuses or interests me. Oh, pardon me, Maurice—I am so rude!' she added, on perceiving the sombre fury expressed by his sinister face.

'Whatever you think, only say that you will be sorry when I go,' he urged.

'If you do go—which I don't believe—-I will be sorry of course, Maurice,' she replied, as she saw the necessity of temporising a little; 'I am always so when I lose anyone or anything that has become familiar to me. Do you not remember how I wept when my poor Bologna spaniel died last year?'

'I do not expect you to weep for me. It would be

too much for Maurice Morganstjern to expect to be raised to the level of your spaniel.'

'How sarcastic and unpleasant you are!' exclaimed Dolores, expectant of Lewie Baronald's arrival, and now half dreading that event. 'I wish you would be as faithful as that poor animal was, and as unselfish in your love.'

'Could you look into my heart, you would find but one word—one idea stamped there.'

'And that is——'

'"Dolores"—meaning sorrow and lamentation if you love me not.'

She laughed merrily again, and again the sombre look came into his face; so she dropped her fan and held out two small white hands as if to deprecate his wrath, for she had an energetic way with her, so he instantly caught them in his own.

She was quite occupied in trying to release them when a familiar rap was heard on the knocker of the street door, an enormous lion's head of brass, with a huge ring in its jaws.

'Oh, I keep your hands prisoners,' said he : 'pardon me,' he added, as he stooped and kissed them ; and she had barely time to wrench them away when a liveried valet ushered in Lewie Baronald, and in spite of herself and the presence of her cousin she could

not conceal the joy with which his presence inspired
her.

'Welcome,' she said, and held forth her hand. Oh,
what a hand he thought it—small, plump, and white
—so slim and shapely !

There was neither shyness, coquetry, nor embarrass-
ment in the girl's manner, for in their assured position with each other both she and her lover were long
past anything of the kind ; but the latter and her cousin
bowed rather grimly to each other, and mutually
muttered :

'Your servant—Mynheer.'

Lewie Baronald now crossed the polished floor of
the drawing-room to greet the Countess, who rose to
receive him, and who looked so young and so pretty
that she might have passed for an elder sister of
Dolores ; and stooping low he kissed her hand, looking,
as he did so, with his sword at his side under the stiff
square skirt of his coat, and his hat under his arm,
with his ruffles and cravat of fine lace, a model of
those stately manners that lingered in Europe when
George III. was King—in Scotland, perhaps, longer
than anywhere else.

Of Morganstjern's privileges as a cousin, Lewie
Baronald was never jealous in the least ; but on this
occasion, after the recent fencing-bout, the interview

with his uncle, and the threat of service in the Dutch West Indies, his brow was rather cloudy, and he longed intensely to be with Dolores alone.

The rough sword-play that had been forced upon him, the risk he had run, and the treachery of Morganstjern, had certainly exasperated him ; but courtesy to Dolores and the Countess made him dissemble, and he treated his rival and enemy, if rather coldly and haughtily, as if nothing remarkable had occurred between them, and the conversation became of a general kind. But Morganstjern, in the waspishness of his nature, could not help referring to the 'armed neutrality,' as it was termed, a vexed and then danger-ous political subject for a Briton and a Hollander to discuss.

This was an alliance, offensive and defensive, which had been formed by some of the northern powers of Europe ; and some violent disputes between Britain and the States-General, which seemed advancing to a direct rupture just then, caused the position of the Scots Brigade in their service to become somewhat peculiar and critical.

From the commencement of the disturbance with America, the Dutch had maintained a close corre-spondence with the revolted colonists, supplying them with all kinds of material and warlike stores ; and

after the interference of France and Spain, the selfish-
ness and treachery of the Dutch became more glaring
and apparent.

'The States-General of Holland are free, independent, and can do precisely as they choose,' said
Morganstjern haughtily, in reply to some condem-
natory remark of Lewie Baronald.

'Their Highnesses,' replied the latter calmly, 'have
no right to leave their ports open to the King's rebels,
in disregard of friendship and honour, and in defiance
of the remonstrances of his ambassadors.'

'Permit me to dispute your right, as a soldier in
the service of their Highnesses, to censure them.'

Baronald's nether lip quivered at this retort, and
the Countess and Dolores exchanged glances of
uneasiness; for politics had become so embittered
by the American Squadron, which had recently captured H.M.'s ships *Serapis* and *Scarborough*, having
taken them into the Texel, and when General Yorke
claimed those ships and their crews, the Dutch
refused to restore them, and soon after Commodore
Fielding fired upon their squadron under Count
Bylandt, and took him into Portsmouth; so war was
looked for daily, while the Scots Brigade were yet
serving under the Dutch colours.

'Do not let us think or speak of such things, Cousin

Maurice,' said Dolores imploringly; 'I tremble at the idea of Britain invading us, if this sort of work goes on. What have we to do with her colonists and their quarrels?'

'Invade us, indeed!' said Morganstjern, with angry mockery; 'if our swords fail us we can open the sluices, as we did in the days of Louis XIV., and drown every man and mother's son!'

'But how should we escape ourselves?' asked the Countess.

'Good generalship would take care of that; and then how about your Scots Brigade?' asked Morganstjern, turning abruptly to Baronald.

'The Bulwark of Holland, we have never failed her yet,' replied the latter haughtily; 'but to draw the sword upon our own countrymen is certainly a matter for consideration.'

'In Holland, perhaps, but not in America.'

'Let this subject cease,' said the Countess imperatively, while fanning herself with an air of excessive annoyance; and now Morganstjern, beginning to find himself *de trop*, bowed himself out, and with vengeance gathering in his heart, withdrew to an estaminet, or tavern, where he knew that he would find his friend the Heer van Schrekhorn, and whither we may perhaps follow him.

To Lewie Baronald, who was naturally destitute of much personal vanity, it had hitherto seemed rather strange that the Countess had permitted his attentions to her daughter at all, though he was known to be the heir of his uncle; and now that he had all the joy of knowing himself to be her accepted lover, his soul trembled within him at the prospect of having to announce General Kinloch's utter hostility to the mother.

Lewie had more than once observed that the Countess always smiled, or laughed outright, when his uncle the General was spoken of, as if she considered him somewhat of a character—an *excentrique*.

'You have seen the General, I presume, since you were here last?' said she.

'Yes, madam,' replied Lewie, painfully colouring.

'And told him of your love for Dolores— of your engagement to her, in fact?'

'Yes, madam; he seems to have suspected it for some time past.'

'Suspected—that sounds unpleasant.'

Lewie played with the feather in his regimental hat, and his colour deepened, when the Countess said :

'Then he is coming to wait upon me, I presume?'

'Alas—no, madam.'

'Indeed—why?'

'He is averse to the society of ladies.'

'In fact, is a woman-hater, I have heard.'

Lewie smiled feebly, and felt himself in a foolish predicament; so the Countess spoke again.

'He had some disappointment in early life, I believe, and never got over it.'

'Yes, madam.'

'Poor fellow! and of Dolores——'

'He will not hear me speak with patience.'

'How grotesque!' exclaimed the Countess, laughing heartily.

'Ah, could he but see her!' exclaimed the young man, regarding the upturned face of her he loved with something of adoration.

'Your uncle the General is very cruel, Lewie,' said Dolores; 'he is a veritable ogre!'

'He is the king of good fellows, but——'

'But what?'

'He has never seen you.'

'And never shall,' she said petulantly, opening and shutting her fan.

'Nay, dearest Dolores, do not say so.'

'The ogre, or worse!' exclaimed the girl, with a pout on her sweet lips.

'Nay—no worse—only a man,' said the Countess, laughing excessively; 'he thinks of us only as

women, but to be shunned—avoided—dreaded. It is
very droll!'

And looking down, she played with the *étui* and
appendages that hung from her girdle, her tiny watch
with the judgment of Solomon embossed on its case;
and as she did so, Lewie thought her hand as white
and dimpled as that of Dolores.

To him it certainly seemed strange that the opposition of his uncle seemed only to provoke—not the
pride or the indignation of the lively Countess—but
her laughter and amusement.

'And if he gets me banished on foreign service
to the Dutch West Indies!' he urged rather
piteously.

'My poor Lewie,' said she, patting his cheek with
her fan, 'I must see what can be done; meantime,
we must be patient and wait. From all I have heard
and know, an early disappointment at the hands of
one he loved only too well, has shaken his faith in
human goodness and integrity, and now he is soured,
suspicious and sarcastic.'

'But only so far as women are concerned.'

'True; and I suppose he is like a French writer,
who says that "of all serious things, marriage is the
most ridiculous;" but men are not infallible, especially
men like your uncle the General—*errare humanum*

est. Let us be patient a little, and all will come right in the end.'

But Dolores and her lover would only sigh a little impatiently as her hand stole into his, and the twilight of evening deepened around them.

CHAPTER V.

'THE BULWARK OF HOLLAND.'

AND now while the lovers are waiting in hope, while the General is 'nursing his wrath to keep it warm,' and determined upon their separation; and while Maurice Morganstjern is plotting what mischief he may work them, we shall briefly tell the story of the Scots Brigade, and how it came to be called 'the Bulwark of Holland.'

Lewie Baronald, his uncle the General, and all others belonging to the Scots Brigade, had a good right to be proud of doing so, as it had a glorious inheritance of military history, second only to that of the 1st Royal Scots; and though its memory should have been immortal, its records now lie rotting in a garret

of the Town House of Amsterdam ; and even in
Scotland little is remembered of it, save its march :

> ' The Lowlands o' Holland
> Hae parted my love and me.'

Yet the drums of that Brigade have stirred the
echoes of every city and fortress between the mouths
of the Ems in the stormy North Sea, and the oak
forests of Luxembourg and the Ardennes ; and
between the ramparts of Ostend and the banks of
the Maese and Rhine.

In 1570 the fame of Maurice, Prince of Nassau,
drew to his standard many of those Scots whose
swords were rendered idle by peace with England,
and it was by their aid chiefly, that he drove out his
Spanish invaders.   Among those who took with
them the bravest men of the Borders, were that Sir
Walter Scott of Buccleugh who exasperated Queen
Elizabeth by storming the Castle of Carlisle ; his son
Walter, the first Earl of Buccleugh ; Sir Henry
Balfour of Burleigh ; Preston of Gourton ; Halkett
of Pitfiran, and other commanders, named by Grose,
Stewart, Hay, Douglas, Graham, and Hamilton.

These formed the original Scots Brigade in the
army of Holland, and some of the battalions must
have been kilted, as Famiano Strada, the Jesuit,

states that at the battle of Mechlin they fought 'naked'—*nudi pugnant Scoti multi.*

In 1594, on the return of the States ambassadors, whither they had gone to congratulate James VI. on the birth of his son, they took back with them 1,500 recruits for the Brigade, which five years after fought valiantly in repelling the Spaniards at the siege of Bommel.

The year 1600 saw its soldiers cover themselves with glory at the great battle of the Downs, near Nieuport, and in the following year at the siege of Ostend, which lasted three years, and in which 100,000 men are said to have perished on both sides, and where so many of Spinola's bullets 'stuck in the sandhill bulwark that it became like a wall of iron, and dashed fresh bullets to pieces when they hit it;' and so great was the valour of the Brigade at the siege of Bois-le-Duc, that Frederick Henry, Prince of Orange, styled it 'The Bulwark of the Republic.'

It consisted then of three battalions—those of Buccleugh, Scott, and Halkett.

The bestowal of some commissions on Dutch officers caused much discontent during the time of the Prince of Orange, afterwards William III., with whom (after being demanded by James VII. without effect in 1688) the Brigade came over to Britain for a time, and

served at the siege of Edinburgh Castle and the battle
of Killiecrankie.

In 1747, by the slaughter at Val and the terrible
siege of Bergen-op-Zoom, the Brigade was reduced to
only 330 men, but the *Hague Gazette* records how they
drove the French from street to street, and of all the
glory won thus, the greatest fell to two lieutenants
named Maclean, the sons of the Laird of Torloisk,
who were complimented by Count Lowendhal, who
commanded the enemy, by whom they were taken.

The men of the Brigade were ever good soldiers,
yet strict and God-fearing Presbyterians, who would
rather have had their peccadilloes known to a stern
General like Kinloch, than to the regimental chaplain.

And it might be said of this Brigade, as it used to
be said of the Scots Greys, that the members of it
retained a kind of regimental dialect coeval with the
days of its formation, when the language was rather
different from the present Scotch; so, in the Irish
brigades of France and Spain the strongest and
purest old Irish was found to the last.

As a sequel to this brief account of the Brigade in
Holland, we may sum up the story of its service in
the British army—though that service was brilliant—
in little more than a paragraph.

After a long and angry correspondence between the

Governments of Holland and Britain, the Brigade—save some fifty officers who had formed ties in Holland, or elected to remain there—was transferred to the service of the latter, when a rupture took place between them at the time of the American War, and was taken to Edinburgh, clad in the Dutch uniform, and about 1794, it adopted the red coat, and there in George's Square, when drawn up under Generals Dundas and Kinloch, received its new colours at the hands of the Scottish Commander-in-Chief, when it was numbered as the 94th Regiment ; and under these colours it fought gallantly at Seringapatam, winning the elephant as a badge ; at the storming of Ciudad Rodrigo, and in all the battles of the Peninsular War, after which it was disbanded at Edinburgh in 1818.

Then another 94th was embodied five years afterwards, on which occasion, as we tell in our novel, ' The King's own Borderers,' ' the green standard of the old Brigade of immortal memory was borne through the streets from the Castle of Edinburgh by a soldier of the Black Watch,' thus identifying the new regiment with the old ; but now even the number of the former has passed away, as under the new and helplessly defective army organisation scheme, it is muddled up with the 88th Regiment under a new name.

And now, having told what the 'Bulwark of Holland' was, we shall return to the fortunes of Lewie Baronald and his *fiancée* Dolores.

CHAPTER VI.

AT THE GOLDEN SUN.

'So—so! this Scottish adventurer stands between me and the girl I love; between me and my own flesh and blood; more than all, between me and the fortune of Dolores!' muttered Morganstjern—himself a penniless adventurer and knave to boot, as he strode through the streets with his left hand in the hilt of his sword and his right tightly clenched. 'I have a right to hate and dread him—the right to remove him, too, by fair means or foul!'

The latter were the only means he could think of, as he had a wholesome dread of Lewie Baronald's skill with his sword, and the bucks of the Scots Brigade were not wont to stand on trifles when they resorted to that weapon; and in this mood of mind he rejoined his friend the Heer van Schrekhorn, whom he found at an estaminet called the *Goud Zon*, or

'Golden Sun,' in a narrow and gloomy street near the Klooster Kerk.

There he found him seated in a quiet corner, smoking, drinking schiedam and water, while intently studying some profitable and useful gambling tricks with a pack of not overclean cards.

'I have just been trying some ruses or tricks at lansquenet,' said he, as the tapster brought fresh glasses and more liquor ; 'it is the grandest of old gambling games, like those that are of French origin. Look here, to begin with : the cards being shuffled by the dealer, and cut by one of the party, two are dealt out and turned up on the left hand of the dealer, *so ;* he then takes one and places a fourth, the *réjouissance* card, in the middle of the table, *so.* On this——'

'Enough of this, Van Schrekhorn,' said Morganstjern impatiently. 'I did not come here to be taught lansquenet,' he added, as he threw his sword, hat, and gloves on a side-table, and flung himself wearily into a chair.

'Oh—so you have just come from the house of *la belle* Dolores ?'

' Yes,' replied the other with an imprecation.

'And left her well and happy, I hope ?' said the Heer mockingly.

'I left her with that fellow of the Scots Brigade.'

' 'Sdeath! the more fool you. Why not keep your
ground? Were you not there before him?'

' Yes, and did my best to win her favour—even her
mere regard.'

' In vain?'

' As usual. In fact, I think these two are affianced
—or nearly so. I never so bestirred myself about a
woman before,' said Morganstjern, as he drank at a
draught a crystal goblet of schiedam and water, and
refilled it.

' How is the Countess affected towards you?'

' But indifferently. Indeed, she only tolerates me
as a kinsman, and, I suppose, has encouraged or permitted Baronald's addresses to her daughter, because
he is the heir of General Kinloch, while I am heir to
that only of which nothing can deprive me.'

' And that is?'

' A grave—six feet of earth,' replied Morganstjern,
grinding his teeth unpleasantly.

' Come—you have always the guilders you win at
roulette.'

' Because they are so won, there is the greater
necessity that I should have those of my cousin
Dolores.'

' Which also reminds me that you owe me a good
sum of money—cash lent, and lost at play.'

'Why the devil remind me of that just now?' replied, or rather asked, Morganstjern, savagely; and then for a little time the two smoked moodily in silence.

The would-be lover of Dolores had long been subjected to a run of evil fortune at the gaming-table. 'So long as there is the beacon of hope,' says a writer, 'life is able to show up a gleam now and then of rose-colour; but when adverse circumstances render any change *impossible*, life becomes intolerable.' And to this verge of desperation had Maurice Morganstjern come.

It was a source of keen irritation to him, to find that his rival—favoured by the Countess—could be with Dolores daily, while he—her cousin—could only visit her at stated times; and that all the advances he made to her seemed utterly futile and hopeless now.

'Nearly penniless as I am, Schrekhorn,' said he; 'I might have waited patiently, but have never had a gleam of hope.'

'If you waited a hundred years, it would be all the same, while she is under the influence of this fellow's voice, eye, and society.'

'What would you have me do?'

'Remove him, or remove her!' replied Schrekhorn with a fierce Dutch oath.

' More easily said than done. With her money, by the henckers! how I should enjoy myself all day long and do nothing!'

' About all you ever cared to do,' rejoined his friend, who was rather disposed to treat him mockingly.

' Don't attempt to act my Mentor.'

' Why ?'

' Because I should make but a sorry Telemachus.'

' Then it seems all a settled thing between them !'

' What ?'

' How dull you are ! Marriage ?'

' Ach Gott! it looks like it.'

' Then you have been a trifle late of taking the field ?'

' Nay,' replied Morganstjern, smoking his meerschaum with vicious energy. ' I was the first, but when this fellow Baronald came, I found myself instantly at a discount.'

' Jilted—ch ?'

' Nay, I was never on such a footing with her that she could treat me so, because she was ever utterly indifferent.'

' Then it is too late for fair means now, but not for foul.'

Then, after a pause, the Heer said in his mocking tone :

'If money is your object, and you openly avow that it is so, why not propose to the mother, if the daughter won't have you? She is rich enough and certainly handsome enough, and only some fifteen years older than yourself. She is a widow, and all the world knows how easily widows are won. 'Sblood! cut in for her, and leave the girl to the Scot.'

Morganstjern thought for a minute, and then uttering one of his imprecations, added:

'No—*no*—NO! I shall be thwarted by no man!'

'Right!' exclaimed the other; 'I like this spirit—give me your hand.'

'This infernal Scots Brigade has married at the Hague and Amsterdam more than fifty Dutch girls within the last few years, and all of them rich.'

'Der Duyvel!'

'Many of them girls of the first rank.'

'Thousand duyvels!' said the Heer with a mocking laugh.

'Is it not enough that these Scots—the Bulwark of the Republic as they boast themselves——'

'And have done so since the old siege of Bois-le-Duc—well?' asked the Heer.

'Is it not enough, I say, that they should assume our glory in war, and win our guilders in peace, but they must carry off our prettiest girls too?'

'They do not assume *your* glory, but win their own,' said the Heer, who had some contempt for his companion; 'their guilders have been hardly won on many a Dutch and Flemish battlefield; and if the pretty girls of Haarlem and the Hague prefer them to Walloons, they are right.'

Morganstjern's brow grew black.

'I am no Walloon,' said he, huskily.

'I did not say so,' said Van Schrekhorn; then he added, 'I have some news for you, and a hint to make thereon. Dolores van Renslaer is to be at the ridotto given by the wife of the Sixe van Otterbeck, the Minister of State, on the night after next.'

'That I know, and of course this pestilent Scot will be there too.'

'No; on that night he is on duty at the Palace of the Prince of Orange.'

'Well—what about all this?'

'Listen,' said Van Schrekhorn, leaning forward on the table and lowering his voice almost to a whisper, while the colour in his bloated visage deepened, and an expression of intense cunning stole into his watery bloodshot eyes: 'let us carry her off as her sedan bears her from the ridotto!'

'To where?'

'Listen. I know a skipper whose ship is now in

the Maese, and almost ready to sail for the coast of France. She is anchored off Macsluis now ; let us once get her on board and the Hoek van Holland will soon be left astern, and the girl your own, unless you are a greater fool than I think you.'

Morganstjern made no immediate reply, so his tempter spoke again.

'Once on board that ship, her honour will be compromised, and marriage alone can restore it. Let her be once on board that ship with you, I say, and she cannot be so blind as not to see that she will have gone a great deal too far to draw back.'

'Right!' exclaimed Morganstjern, as a glance of triumph came into his eyes. 'I have a political mission to France, and it will be supposed that she has eloped with me, and befooled the Scot Baronald. With all her contempt and scorn of me, she little knows that her fate is to become my wife—my wife— *mine!* Once that, and then let her look to herself!' he added as a savage expression mingled with the triumph that sparkled in his shifty eyes, and he smote the table with his clenched hand.

'The distance from the Hague to Macsluis is only eleven miles—a few pipes, as the people say,' resumed Schrekhorn ; 'my friend shall have a boat waiting us at a quiet spot among the willows that fringe the shore, near a deserted windmill on the river-bank ; and then we shall take her on board. Once under hatches, her fate will soon be sealed.'

' How can I thank you ?'

' By refunding what you owe me out of the guilders of Dolores,' replied the Heer, as he and Morganstjern shook hands again ; but the latter became silent for a time.

He knew the Heer van Schrekhorn to be a rascal capable of committing any outrage, and also that he had personally a special grudge at Lewie Baronald. Dolores was beautiful. What if this scheme so speciously arranged, was one for his own behoof, to carry her off, leaving the onus of the abduction on the shoulders of him—Morganstjern—after passing a sword through his body among the willows near the old mill on the Maese.

But this grave suspicion was only a passing thought, and he thrust it aside.

' This may preclude your return for some time, and compromise you with the authorities,' said the Heer.

' Their reign will soon be over ; and when a French army comes to the assistance of the Dutch patriots, the Prince of Orange may find himself a fugitive in England.'

' But we must be wary ; not for all the gold and

silver bars in the Bank of Amsterdam would I be in your shoes if we fail. The Burgomasters are worse than the devil to face, and we may find ourselves behind the grilles of the Gevangepoort or the Rasphaus, as brawlers.'

'A thousand duyvels!—fail? don't think of it.'

Had Maurice Morganstjern known the intentions of General Kinloch towards his nephew, and the plans he had formed to separate him from Dolores, he might have patiently awaited the events of the next few days; but as he was ignorant of them, he and the malevolent Heer van Schrekhorn laid all their plans for the abduction of the girl with caution, confidence, and extreme deliberation, before they quitted the Golden Sun that night.

CHAPTER VII.

THE GENERAL'S SECRET.

NEXT day, when Lewie Baronald, apparelled in all his regimental bravery, was setting forth to visit Dolores, he was summoned by General Kinloch, who, after working himself up to a certain degree of sternness or firmness, real or assumed, for the occasion, said :

'Stay, young man, I pray you, as we must have some conversation together.'

Lewie took off his Khevenhüller hat, and fearing that some animadversions were coming, played a little irresolutely with its upright scarlet feather.

'Your name has gone in for foreign service, Lewie,' said the General.

'To whom, sir ?'

'The Director-General of Infantry.'

'Sent by you, uncle ?'

'Yes, sir, by me.'

'You might at least have consulted with me in this matter. How cruel of you, uncle, under all the circumstances !' exclaimed Lewie, with sudden bitterness and intense anger.

'You will come to think it kindness in time, boy ; I seek but to save you from what I, in my time, underwent.'

'If I refuse to go ?'

'Refuse, and compromise your honour and mine —yea, the honour of the Brigade itself ! My dear Lewie, when you have lived in this world as long as I——'

'Why, uncle, you are only forty !'

'Not yet twice your age, certainly—well?'

'If detailed for the Colonies, anywhere, separation from Dolores will be the death of me!' exclaimed the young man passionately.

'No, it won't; nor of Dolores either. So you are very much in love with her?' asked the General with a scornful grin.

'God only knows how purely I love her!' exclaimed the nephew in a low concentrated voice.

'Nature is full of freaks, certainly!'

'How?'

'She has varied the annals of the old fighting line of the Baronalds of that Ilk, by having them varied by something else.'

'By what?'

'A moonstruck fool!'

'This is eccentricity combined with unwarrantable interference and military tyranny,' cried Lewie, as he stuck his hat on his head and drew himself haughtily up; then in a moment his mood changed, for he loved this kinsman to whom he owed so much, and he said with an air of dejection, 'How shall I ever tell Dolores of what you have done to us both? I cannot sail for the Cape or the Caribbean Isles, and leave her bound to me! I must release her from her promise, though I know that she would wait a lifetime for me.'

'Poor fool that you are, Lewie! Do you forget the adage, "Out of sight, out of mind"? You think that, like Penelope, she will wait your return in hope, in love, and all the rest of it? You may be like Ulysses, but never was there a Penelope among women.'

The General indulged in many more doubting and slighting remarks upon women, particularly on their faith and constancy; and while he was running on thus, grief struggled with rage and indignation for mastery in the heart of Lewie, which seemed to stand still at this sudden wrench, and the prospect of an abrupt and protracted separation from Dolores—a separation that might be for years—every moment of which would be an agonised heart-throb, it seemed to him then!

How hard, how cruel, that they should be thus separated, and forced to drink, as it were, of the bitter waters of Marah, because this stern soldier hated all women so grotesquely, as the Countess had said, viewing them all through the medium of *one;* while Lewie and Dolores were so young that all the world seemed too small to contain the measure of their joy, and now—now, thought was maddening!

He would resign, ' throw up his pair of colours,' as the phrase was then ; but his uncle had compromised him, by sending in his name to the Director-General of Infantry !

Already in anticipation he imagined and rehearsed their parting ; already he saw her tears, her blanched face, and heard himself entreating her not to forget him, while vowing himself to be true to her—each regarding the other mournfully and yearningly, hand clasped in hand, lip clinging to lip ; then came the void of the departure ; the seas to plough, and the years that were to come with all their doubts and longing.

It was too bad—too bad ; he owed his uncle much —all in the world indeed ; but this stroke—this harsh interference, ended all between them for ever !

Overwhelmed with dejection he cast himself into a chair ; there the General regarded him wistfully, and placing a hand kindly on his shoulder, said :

'Lewie, shall I tell you of what once happened to me ?'

But, full of his own terrible thoughts, Lewie made no reply.

'It may have been that evil followed me,' said the General, looking down, with a hand placed in the breast of his coat.

'Evil ?' repeated Lewie.

'Yes. When a boy I shot in the wood of Thomineau the last crane that was ever seen in Scotland, and my old nurse predicted that a curse would follow me therefor ; thus, I never see a crane on a house-top here that I don't remember her words. Now listen to what happened to me when I was on de-tachment in the Dutch West India Islands. I belonged then to the battalion of Charles Halkett Craigie, who six years ago died Lieutenant-Governor of Namur, and we garrisoned Fort Nassau, or New Amsterdam as it is called now. There,' continued the General, alternately and nervously toying with his sword-knot and shirt-frill, ' I was silly enough to fall in love with the daughter of a wealthy merchant, a Dutch girl, like your Dolores, with some of the old Castilian blood in her, though a lineal descendant of the great Dutch family of Van Peere, to whom, in 1678, Berbice was granted by the States-General as a perpetual and hereditary fief. She possessed great beauty, and what proved more attractive still, a hundred sweet and winning ways, with the art of saying pretty and even daring little things, that endeared her to all—to none more than me. I was a great ass, of course ; but, heavens, what a coquette she was !'

' What was her name ?' asked Lewie, with just the smallest amount of interest.

'Excuse me telling, as I have sworn never to utter it again ; nor do I wish it to go down in the annals of our family. She wound herself round my heart ; my soul, my existence, seemed to be hers. My love for her became a species of idolatry ; but poverty tied my tongue, and I dared not speak of it, till one evening, which I shall never forget, the secret left me abruptly, drawn from me by *herself.* We were lingering in the garden of her father's villa near the Berbice river, and the stars were coming out, one by one, in the deep blue sky above us. The hour was beautiful—all that a lover could wish ; and around us the atmosphere was fragrant with the perfume of flowers— among those wonders of the vegetable world—the gigantic water-lilies, each leaf of which is six feet in diameter. I was soon to leave for Holland on duty, and my heart was wrung at the prospect of a separation.

'I had her hand in mine : my secret was trembling on my lips ; and gazing into her eyes which were of a golden-brown colour, like that of her hair, I said very softly :

'"If your eyes have at all times an expression so sweet, so beautiful and winning, what must they seem to the man who reads love in them—love for himself !"

'"Can you not read it now?" she asked in a low voice, as she cast her long lashes down.

'I uttered her name and drew her close to me, my heart beating wildly the while, in doubt whether this was one of the daring little speeches I spoke of.

'Taking her sweet little face between my hands, I kissed her eyes and forehead, on which she said, in her low cooing voice:

'"I wonder if you will ever think of me after you are gone?"

'"Darling, do you think there will ever be a day of my life when I will *not* think you! Oh, the thought of our parting is worse than death to me!"'

('A fellow feeling makes us wondrous kind,' thought Lewie, becoming fully interested now.)

'"We are jesting," said she; "do not say this."

'"There is no need to tell you that I love you," said I, "for you know that I do—dearly, fondly: that this love will last with life, end with death;" and much more rubbish I said to the same purpose, adding, "And you, if quite free, could you love me?"

'"I love you now; have I not admitted as much?"

'So it all came about in that way,' said the General; 'umph—what an ass I was! May you never live to be deceived as that girl deceived me! I thought our passion was mutual; and then perhaps she thought so too—all perfidious though she was!

'But how happy—how radiantly happy I was for a time, till a Dutch squadron came to anchor off the bar of the Berbice river, and in one of the lieutenants thereof she discovered, or said she discovered, a kinsman; and from that moment a blight fell upon me, and I discovered that she was variable as the wind. Her attentions seemed divided for a time; at last they were no longer given to me. Her smiles were for the stranger; she sang to him, played to him, and talked to him only. At home or abroad, riding or driving, or boating on the river, he was ever by her side when not on board his ship.

'What rage and mortification were in my heart! The rules of the service alone prevented me calling him to a terrible account, though indeed he was not to blame.

'When I attempted to reason or remonstrate with her, she laughed; then after a time became indignant. We parted in anger, and I felt fury and death in my heart when she tossed my engagement-ring at my feet.

'Once again we met, alone, and by the merest chance. How my pulses throbbed as our eyes met, and she coyly presented her hand, which I was craven enough, and fool enough, to fondle!

' " Oh, what have I done," said I, " that you should treat me thus ? that you should tread my heart under your feet, and leave me to long years of sorrow and repining ?"

' Then she laughed, and snatched her hand away, while once again my soul seemed to die within me.

' " Do you love this kinsman ?" I asked her fiercely ; and never till my last hour shall I forget her reply, or the almost cruel expression of her face.

' " Yes ; I love him—love him with my whole heart, and as I never loved you !"

' Turning away, she left me—left me rooted to the spot. Yet she had some shame, or compunction, left in her after all ; for next day came a would-be piteous letter of explanation, that she had given this lieutenant a promise to please her father when he was dying—her father who was his guardian ; how she had never had the courage to tell me so at first; that she did not dream I loved her so much ; that I must learn to forget her, though she would never forget me ; and so—a thousand devils !—there was an end of it.

' A few weeks after I saw her marriage in the papers, to the Lieutenant—d——n his name—to her and her fortune of ever so many thousand guilders.

' I tore her farewell letter into minute fragments, and set to work to adopt her advice,'

'What was that?' asked Lewie.

'To forget her; and to do so I threw myself into my profession. I never looked upon her face again, and I thanked God when I heard our drums beating as we marched out of Fort Nassau, and when the accursed shore of the Berbice river faded into the evening sea! Now, Lewie, have I not the best of reasons for mistrusting women, and seeking to save you from the fangs of this little ogress—this Dolores?'

'Ah, you know not her of whom you speak thus!' exclaimed Lewie.

'Nor am I likely to do so. Shun her, nephew! a girl, doubtless, with a fair face, and a heart as black as Gehenna! Be firm, Lewie Baronald!—firmness is a great thing, as you will find when you come to be a general officer and as old as I am.'

Lewie had done his duty like a man and a soldier—like one worthy of the glorious old Brigade—among the savages in the old Cape War; but it was cruel, absurd, and, to use the Countess van Renslaer's phrase, 'grotesque,' that he should now be treated like a child, and in the most momentous matter of his life and happiness too!

'I was weak enough—idiot enough, to wish I might die, then and there, when that girl deceived me,' resumed his uncle bitterly; 'but I knew that I must live on and on; I was very young, and thought I might live for forty years with that pain in my heart at night and in the morning. It is twenty years since then, and though the pain is dead, I suppose, I cannot laugh at it yet, or the memory of Mercedes.'

'Mercedes! was that her name—Mercedes?'

'The devil—it has escaped me!'

'So that is the name which is not to go down in the annals of the family?'

'Precisely so.'

'But surely, dear uncle, after all these years, you must have forgiven her? Besides, she may be dead.'

'Dead to me, certainly! Forgiven her—well, perhaps I may have forgiven her; but what can make a mere mortal forget a wrong, a cruelty, or an injury?'

'Then you will not yield, but insist that I shall go abroad?'

'I will not yield an inch, and march you shall!, replied the General, as he turned on his heel and left him.

'My darling Dolores—the first and only love of my life!' exclaimed the young man passionately; 'how can he—how *dare* he—act thus towards us? But that I love him, I think, I may soon come to hate him!'

He rushed away in search of Dolores; but she and

the Countess were from home. He was on duty at the Palace next day, and Dolores was to be at the ridotto ; thus, ere they could meet, events were to transpire which were altogether beyond the conception of both.

CHAPTER VIII.

THE RIDOTTO.

THE 'ridotto,' the Italian word then fashionable for an entertainment of music and dancing, at the huge old red-brick villa of the Heer van Otterbeck, Minister of State, in the vicinity of the Hague, was one of the gayest affairs of the season.

The Prince of Orange (whose son afterwards became King of the Netherlands) was not present, but all the rank, the wealth, and beauty of the Hague were represented ; and among those present were many officers of the Scots Brigade, including the Earl of Drumlanrig, General Dundas, in after years the captor of the Cape of Good Hope ; and there too was the Conservator of Scottish Privileges at Campvere,

John Home, then the celebrated author of the nearly
forgotten tragedy of 'Douglas.'

A band of the Dutch Guards furnished music on the
lawn, and there dancing was in progress in the bright
sunshine of the summer afternoon ; and, in the fashion
of the time, many of the guests were arrayed in what
they deemed the costume of Arcadian shepherds and
shepherdesses.

People danced early in the evenings of the eighteenth
century, and were abed about the time their descen-
dants now begin to dress for a ball. Ices were unknown ; no wine was dispensed, but the liveried
servants of the Heer van Otterbeck regaled his guests
on coffee, green tea, orange tea, and many kinds of
cakes and confectionery in the intervals of the
dancing, in which Dolores (all innocent and unaware of the plots in progress against her peace,
even her honour and liberty—one of them born of
avarice, wounded vanity, and foiled desire) indulged
joyously and with all her heart.

For the information of the ladies of the present day
we shall detail the dress worn by Dolores on that
evening as described in the *Hague Gazette*, and they
may imagine how charming she looked :

'Her body and train were silver tissue, with a broad
silver fringe ; her petticoat was white satin covered

with the richest crape, embroidered with silver, fastened up with bunches of silver roses, tassels, and
cords. Her pocket-holes were blonde, her stockings
were blue, clocked with silver, and her hair was twisted
and plaited in the most beautiful manner around a
diamond comb.'

Seated under a tree, flushed with a recent dance, she
was alternately playing with her fan and silver
pomander ball, with a crowd of admirers about her,
and looking alike pure and bright, with 'a skin as
though she had been dieted on milk and roses.'

'No wonder it is, perhaps, that Lewie loves me,'
thought the girl, as she looked at the reflection of her
own sweet face in a little bit of oval mirror in the
back of her huge Dutch fan; 'I *am* pretty!'

She might have said ' lovely,' and more than lovely ;
and then she smiled consciously at her own vanity.

Under the genial influence of her surroundings the
heart of the girl was full of happiness, and had but
one regret that Lewie Baronald was not there. Yet,
she thought, ' to-morrow I shall see him--to-morrow
be with my darling, who at this moment is thinking
of me.'

And amid the brilliance of the scene, so rich in the
variety of colour and costume, the strains of the
music and beauty of the old Dutch pleasure-grounds,

she almost longed to be alone, with the grass, the birds, the insects, and the flowers—alone in the sweet summer evening with the perfume of the roses, the jasmine, and the glorious honeysuckle around her.

On one hand, about a mile distant, was the Hague, with all its Gothic spires and pointed gables ; on the other spread the landscape so usual in that country of cheese and butter—church-towers and wind-mills, bright farmhouses, long rows of willow-trees, their green foliage ruffling up white in the passing breeze ; the grassy dykes and embankments, a long continuity of horizontal lines, which seemed so tame and insipid to the mountaineers of the Scots Brigade, and to all but the Dutch themselves.

Among the groups around her, Dolores, as usual now, heard the growing political quarrel between Great Britain and Holland openly and freely discussed, together with the consequent and too probable departure of the Scots Brigade from the latter for ever. That seemed almost a settled thing—a certainty, if the quarrel became an open one, and the probabilities wrung the girl's affectionate heart.

How would all this affect her lover and herself ? Alas ! she knew not that the doom of the former for foreign service was nearly a fixed thing now ! And she was fated to receive her first mental shock that evening, all unwittingly, from the Earl of Drumlanrig, who drew near her, and with the stately manner of the time lifted his hat with one hand, and with the other touched her hand as he bowed over it.

The golden light of the setting sun fell full upon her hair, flecking its bronze with glorious tints, and giving her beauty a brilliance that, to the Earl's appreciative eye, was very striking.

'You look like one of Watteau's beauties, waiting to hear herself addressed in the language of Love,' said the old peer, smiling.

'Love has three languages, my lord,' observed Dolores.

'Three?'

'The pen, the tongue, and the eyes.'

'True; but I am too old to use any of these now,' said the Earl, shaking his powdered head.

'The evening is a lovely one,' observed Dolores, after a pause.

'And the landscape yonder, as it stretches away towards Delft, is wonderfully steeped in sunshine; and but for its flatness——' the Earl paused.

'Your Scottish eyes cannot forgive that,' said Dolores laughing, as she recalled some of Lewie Baronald's complaints on the same subject; 'but people cannot live on scenery.'

'So the great Samuel Johnson has written.'

'Who is he?' asked Dolores.

'A great lexicographer—a wonderful English savant—who believes in a ghost in London, yet discredited the late earthquake at Lisbon. I think I have seen you at the Vyverberg with Lewis Baronald of my battalion; he has the honour of being known to you.'

'He visits us,' replied Dolores, the flower-like tints of her sweet face growing brighter as the Earl spoke.

'He is a fine and handsome fellow, young Baronald; but it is strange that he should wish to quit the Hague when it possesses such peculiar attractions,' said the Earl markedly, and with a courteous bow.

'Quit the Hague!' repeated Dolores, as if she had not heard him aright.

'I do not know whether the desire to do so, has any connection with his uncle's scheme for the recapture or restitution to Holland of the Island of Goree, off the coast of Senegal, in defiance of the old Treaty of Nimeguen, which gave it to France, a scheme which will win him the favour of their Mightinesses; but young Baronald's name was sent, through me this morning, to the Director-General of Infantry, for instant foreign service.'

'Foreign service!' whispered Dolores, in an almost breathless voice, while her white throat gave a sharp nervous gasp, and her long lashes drooped over her beautiful eyes. 'Surely, my lord, this must be some mistake. Lewie—he had no desire to leave Holland. in any way—he dreaded nothing so much as the departure of the Brigade to Britain; and this— this——'

'No mistake, I assure you,' interrupted the Earl, all unaware of the astonishment he was exciting and the pain he was inflicting, and both of which he must have perceived had not the Heer van Otterbeck, fortunately for Dolores, approached at that moment, and tapping and proffering his Sèvres china snuff-box, 'buttonholed' him on the inevitable subjects, the quarrel between Britain and Holland, Paul Jones in the Texel, and Commodore Fielding's conduct in firing on the Dutch fleet in the Channel, which the Commodore did with hearty goodwill.

But for Dolores, the charms of the ridotto had vanished now; and in sore perturbation of spirit and anxiety of heart, she bade her host and hostess a hurried farewell, summoned her sedan, and took her departure homeward.

The lights, the music—the music of Lulli; the *minuet de la cour*, and the gaiety of the ridotto, faded away behind her as the heiress took the somewhat lonely road that led to the villa of her mother.

She was escorted to her sedan by an officer of the Brigade, a friend of Lewie's, who, as he closed the roof of it over her, thought that she looked like—as he vowed to some others—'a lovely queen in wax-work done up in a glass-case.'

CHAPTER IX.

THE ABDUCTORS.

WHAT was this mystery concerning the movements and intentions of Lewie Baronald, on which the Earl of Drumlanrig had so abruptly but unconsciously thrown a light?

When last they met and parted, Lewie had given no hint of any desire for foreign service, and certainly, with the relations then existing between himself and her, it was the last thing to be thought of.

'Oh,' thought Dolores, 'that I were at home to consult mamma on this amazing subject!'

Her bearers seemed to crawl; she narrowly opened and shut her fan again and again in her impatience, and stamped her little foot on the floor of the sedan in her irritation and anxiety.

Yes! that horrid General—that odious uncle, the eccentric woman-hater, was no doubt at the bottom of it, and had thus resolved to separate Lewie from her, and hot tears started to her eyes at the thought.

Though in the immediate vicinity of the Hague, the road was as lonely as those who awaited her thereon could have wished. The blue dome of heaven, a dome studded with diamonds—each itself a world—was overhead; and steady and silvery was the light of the uprisen moon, above the far expanse of the level landscape.

Suddenly Dolores heard the sound of voices; there were threats on one hand and expostulation on the other. The sedan, with a violent jolt, was suddenly deposited on the ground, and its bearers were dashed aside, as she supposed, by foot-pads. Then a shriek of dismay escaped Dolores, when a man, whose face was half-concealed by a crape mask, threw up the roof of the sedan, opened the door and attempted to drag her out by the hand.

She saw another similarly masked, and a caleche, with a pair of horses, close by.

Never dreaming of outrage for a moment, she thought that she must be the victim of some extra-

ordinary mistake, till she recognised the voice of
Maurice Morganstjern, when her alarm and astonishment instantly changed to indignation.

'Maurice,' she exclaimed, 'for whom do you mistake me? What outrage is this?'

'No mistake at all, my pretty cousin; will you
please to take your seat in this caleche?' he replied
deliberately.

'For what purpose?'

'Time will show, beloved Dolores.'

'Loose my hand. I wish none of your fair words;
they are ever hateful and unwelcome to my ear:
more so than ever when you come thus—as you must
be—intoxicated,' she added, believing this to be the
case.

'Beware, cousin—beware! You know how I love
you, and yet you spurn me. Come, Schrekhorn, and
help me to lift her into the caleche. For all the past
bitterness I shall have a sweet revenge; and, Dolores,
you will learn to love me, when you will have none
else in this world to cling to.'

On seeing the Heer van Schrekhorn, of whose
character she had heard something, approach her,
the girl looked wildly round in terror: the road was
lonely; her home was at some distance, yet the lights
in its windows were visible; but no help was nigh.

She now perceived that nothing less than her forcible abduction was daringly intended; but what lay in the future beyond that, she could scarcely realise.

Her first fears returned with double force, for she knew the recklessness of the two men at whose mercy she found herself. How lovely and helpless she looked!

Ruffian and coward though he was, Maurice Morganstjern was a consummate egotist, and her continued indifference and contempt of him had deeply wounded his *amour propre*, and roused a spirit of revenge.

'It is useless to fight against Fate, Cousin Dolores; and Fate decrees that you are to be mine!' said he, firmly grasping her hand.

'Oh that I were a man!' exclaimed Dolores.

'For what purpose?'

'To strike you to the earth for your insolence and daring.'

'In that case I would not seek to carry you off; so, I thank Heaven that you are *not* a man, sweet cousin!' He placed his face close to hers, and lowering his voice, said through his clenched teeth: 'Listen to me, Dolores; you have, I fear, plighted yourself to the Scotsman Baronald in ignorance of yourself, and now I am here to rescue you from the death in life to which your girlish folly would doom you. I will soon teach you to forget that artful interloper, if you ever thought seriously about him, which I cannot believe, and our marriage will alter all your ideas.'

These references to her lover infuriated Dolores, who was a high-spirited girl; but he wound his arms round her despite all her efforts. With all her strength she kept him, however, at arms' length, exclaiming :

' I hate you—oh, how I hate you !'

' Cease this nonsense, cousin ; a day is coming when you will love me as much as you may think you hate me now !'

' And what will cause the change ?' she asked scornfully.

' Marriage.'

' Why waste time thus?' asked the Heer van Schrekhorn, who had not yet spoken, and who listened to all this with manifest impatience and uneasiness ; ' we know not who may come upon us; so into the caleche with her at once !' he added with an oath.

' 'Sdeath, but she is as strong as I am !' exclaimed Morganstjern, as he strove to drag her from the sedan.

Her slender figure stood very erect, and with tiny hands she strove to free herself from his odious grasp ; but the scorn, indignation, and passionate resentment that flashed in her dark eyes and curled her tender lips, now gave place to much of genuine fear of her assailants and how far their daring might carry them, especially when the Heer laid his brutal hands upon her ; and uttering a wild cry she clung to the sedan, and without a resort to extreme violence would not be torn from it.

Meanwhile the driver of the caleche, who was in ignorance of the purpose his employers had in view, looked on somewhat scared, and was thinking of how he might, in the future, be handled by the Burgomaster or other authorities.

Dolores suddenly found her strength give way, and felt about to faint, when she heard a loud and wrathful exclamation as Morganstjern was dashed aside on one hand, Schrekhorn knocked down in a heap on the other, and there towered between her and them a tall military-looking man, wearing a Khevenhüller hat, and having a scarlet roquelaure wrapped round him.

The latter he instantly threw off, and drew his sword, on which the driver of the caleche whipped up his horses, and fled at full speed towards the Hague, leaving his employers to get out of the affair as they best could.

The first impulse of the two conspirators was to unsheath their swords also ; but their second was to pause ere attempting to use them, as they recognised in their assailant an officer of the Scots Brigade, and one of high rank apparently by his gold aiguilette.

'Protect me, sir—save me!' implored Dolores.

'Scoundrels!' exclaimed the new-comer, waving in a circle round her his long straight sword, the blade of which glittered in the moonlight, and at sight of which Morganstjern fairly shrunk back; 'scoundrels, come on if you dare!'

'Accursed fool that I have been to delay as I did!' said Morganstjern.

'An accursed fool indeed!' rejoined the Heer furiously.

'Defend yourselves!' exclaimed the officer, attacking them both at once, and in a moment Morganstjern found his sword twisted out of his hand and flung high in the air by a circular parry, while the Heer was rendered defenceless by a thrust between the bones of his sword-arm, on which they both turned and fled, muttering curses loud and deep.

'Heaven sent you to my aid, sir, just in time,' said Dolores, bursting into tears now; 'another moment, and I should have fainted helplessly in their clutches.'

'These seemed no common brawlers—can you name them?' asked General Kinloch, for he it was, as he sheathed his sword, and lifted his Khevenhüller respectfully.

'I can name them; but would, as yet, rather be excused, sir.'

'Henckers! I should like to see both tied to the *Gesteel Paul'* (*i.e.*, the whipping-post).

The General now found himself face to face, in the bright moonlight, with a young lady of more than ordinary beauty; but, when the expression of her eyes, her thick brown hair, defined eyelashes, and lovely lips reminded him, as he thought, of a face he had known long ago, and loved to look upon; and her voice, too, was so like the voice of that other, coming as it were out of the mists of memory, he grew cold and rigid in manner, as he said:

'I have no desire to penetrate your secret, young lady, if secret there is that leads you to conceal the names of these men.'

'I have no secrets, sir; but one of these assailants is my near kinsman—a cousin,' replied Dolores, a little haughtily.

'Then allow me to have the honour of escorting you home.'

'I thank you, sir; the gate is close by.'

Again the courteous officer lifted his hat, and held it in one hand, while he led Dolores to the iron gate,

which led to the garden-path terminating at the door
of the Countess's villa ; and then bidding her farewell, he turned away, his good opinion of her by no
means increased by her peculiar reticence as to the
names of those from whose outrageous conduct he
had saved her.

'Odd—very !' he muttered ; 'but every woman is
an enigma !'

As he was about to close the iron gate, something
glittering on the gravelled path caught his eye, and it
proved to be a bracelet of considerable value, which
had become injured in the struggle between Dolores
and her assailants, and thus no doubt dropped from
her wrist.

'One of her vain gauds, of course,' muttered the
General ; 'yet why should she not wear such, as all
other female tricksters do?—a pretty creature—a
charming girl, in fact ! But what the devil am I
saying ? with all her prettiness she is no doubt false
as she is fair—Dead Sea fruit, in fact. I shall send
her bauble by my servant to-morrow, and—but no—
egad ! I'll deliver it in person.'

Returning to the door of the villa, the General used
the great knocker, with which—all unknown to him
—the hand of his nephew Lewie Baronald was so
familiar.

CHAPTER X.

THE FAIR WIDOW.

WHILE waiting on the door-step he looked a little contemptuously at the female ornament, though it was suggestive of a slender and a pretty wrist; but suddenly the expression of his face changed. He had either seen that gold bracelet before, or one most strangely like it, with a similar circle of diamonds round a large emerald; it gave him some curious, angry and bitter thoughts.

'Mynheer, did you knock?' asked a servant, rousing him from his reverie; and the General then became aware that the door was open, and a flood of warm light was streaming from a chandelier through a stately entrance-hall beyond.

He made known his errand, asked for the young lady, and was ushered into the drawing-room, which at that moment was untenanted.

Then, as now, the Dutch drawing-room was deemed a kind of sanctum or state-room, entered but seldom, the chief glory of which is always its highly-polished floor; so much so, that in some parts of Holland the visitor is still obliged to take off his shoes, or be very careful how he cleans them before admittance is granted.

In the aspect of the mansion there was much that indicated a substantial account at the Bank of Amsterdam ; but that was as nothing to General Kinloch : he never thought of it.

By the light of a large lamp, the General had only time to remark that on the walls hung some clever and brilliant flower-pieces by De Heem, Huysum, and others, when Dolores stood before him, still clad in the brilliant costume she had worn at the ridotto, and looking radiantly beautiful.

Though surprised by the visit, she was glad to see her preserver so soon again. Her heart was full of intense gratitude for the succour he had afforded her, and she felt conscious that in her confusion and per-turbation of spirit she had not shown enough, or half enough, of gratitude to him ; yet he had saved her from a fate that would have been worse than death.

With a low bow he tendered her the bracelet, with a few well-chosen words of explanation.

'Thank you, dear sir, a thousand times !' she ex-claimed ; 'it was mamma's, and its loss would have grieved me much. To whom am I indebted for all this kindness ?'

'My name is Kinloch—General Kinloch, at your service, Colonel-Commandant of the Scots Brigade,' he replied with another profound old-fashioned bow.

Lewie's uncle—the terrible General—the ogre, as she had been wont to call and deem him ! The breath of poor Dolores was quite taken away with surprise.

'Mamma is a widow,' said she after a pause; 'you must see her and receive her thanks. A widow and very beautiful,' she added in thought, with the hope that the Countess might win the favour of this grim soldier for Lewie and herself.

'A widow,' repeated the General, with an unmistakable grimace, and with ill-suppressed cynicism in his voice ; 'oh, indeed !' and he thought with a writer who says, 'A widow smacks of the charnel-house ; she either did love her husband, or she didn't ; and in either case who would care to be his successor ?'

The Countess at that moment entered the room and came forward with one of her brightest smiles ; but suddenly she paused, and the smile faded out of her beautiful face. Kinloch returned her bow with a startled air, and to the acute eyes of Dolores it seemed that a recognition, that was *no common one*, took place between her mother and the General.

For a time—but a very little time—amid her terror

and dismay at the attack made upon herself, Dolores
had forgotten the Earl of Drumlanrig's startling intelligence about Lewie's departure for foreign service ;
but now the memory of it returned in full force, and
she looked coldly and earnestly yet distrustfully upon
the General as their mutual enemy.

'Mamma,' said she, 'this is the gentleman of whom
I told you, and who saved me from my assailants.'

'My daughter is under the greatest of obligations to
you—how can I thank you, General Kinloch ?' added
the Countess, presenting her hand, which he touched
slightly, but with reluctance and hesitation.

'Mercedes,' said he ; 'you recognise me, then !'

Both were agitated and pale ; but the Countess was
the first to recover herself.

'What—you know each other, and *he* even knows
your name !' exclaimed Dolores with blank astonishment.

Finding a necessity for speaking, the Countess
thanked him for the service so promptly and gallantly
rendered to her daughter, and expressed no small
indignation at the daring of Maurice Morganstjern
and his abettor ; but while she spoke the General
listened to her as one in a dream, while the sorely
puzzled Dolores looked wonderingly on.

The original of the miniature now concealed in a

secret drawer of the Dutch cabinet before referred to, treasured for years through all his alleged misogyny, was again before him.

'It is long since we met,' said the Countess.

'And—parted,' replied the General, in a hard voice.

'You have attained high rank now.'

'I was but a lieutenant in Halkett-Craigie's Battalion, *then*,' said he pointedly.

'Sir, I pray you to be seated,' and he mechanically took the chair indicated by a motion of her pretty white hand; 'you are not much changed since—since——'

'And you are scarcely changed at all.'

In the lovely matron, in ripe and full womanhood, he had recognised her in a moment—the girl of the hidden miniature, the early love of his youth, Mercedes who had deceived him, who had well-nigh broken his heart and embittered his whole existence.

The golden-brown hair his hands had once loved to fondle and toy with, seemed now more golden than ever, as it was sprinkled a little with brown *marchale*, in the fashion of the day ; but Dolores, in advance of it, wore her rich hair without any such doubtful accessory, and simply brushed backward over a low toupee that showed the contour of her low, broad, and beautiful forehead.

Twenty years had come and twenty years had gone since he last looked on them, yet in the eyes of Mercedes was the old subtle influence, in her voice the old subtle power ; and he felt both so keenly—so intensely—that the thrill which passed through the heart of Kinloch amounted to—if we may use a paradox—a joyous pain !

Memories of the past time, by the Berbice river— memories sweet and sad and thrilling—were coming back with strange and curious force ; the past returned, the present fled, and much that both had thought was long since dead, was reawakened within them.

'Mamma!' exclaimed Dolores, with irrepressible impatience and curiosity ; 'you know General Kinloch ! you have met before !'

'Yes, Dolores darling—my heart certainly tells me so,' replied the Countess, colouring deeply.

'Heart!' said the General ; 'madame, the heart is an obsolete organ, in this our eighteenth century.'

'Perhaps it is too late in life to assume you can have any interest in me now ; but if you will not, even once, take my hand kindly in yours, I shall think that it is not wounded love, but wounded pride, that inspires you still.'

The Countess spoke sweetly, and with one of her brightest and most caressing smiles.

He pressed her little hand for a moment; it was a mighty advance for the General to do so, but the touch sent a thrill to his heart, and he thought how absurdly young she looked to be the mother of Dolores!

'Good heavens!' that young lady was thinking, 'wonders will never cease.'

So the courteous gentleman, the brave Scottish soldier who had saved her—Lewie's terrible uncle—was her mother's early lover!

'The past is gone,' said the General gravely and sadly, and making an effort to withdraw, and yet staying nevertheless; 'so let us not tear open an old wound.'

'Pardon, and permit me to heal it, if I can,' said the Countess coquettishly, as she touched his bronzed hand with her lovely lips, and at this touch he trembled; so Dolores, saying something about taking off her ornaments, withdrew and left them, wonder and joy mingling in her heart together, while the General made an effort to appear indifferent, and to speak calmly, an effort in which he, eventually, signally failed.

'It is strange, madame,' said he; 'but I have lived

so completely in camp and caserne, that I knew not that Mercedes—the Mercedes of other days, and the Countess van Renslaer, of whom my nephew speaks so much, were one and the same.'

'My husband, the Lieutenant——'

The General coughed, and said interrupting :

'Whom you preferred to poor John Kinloch of the Scots Brigade—well ?'

'Died soon after succeeding to his title—a Flemish one—and I have been a widow since.'

'All these years ?'

'All these years.'

Her long dark eyelashes flickered as she looked coyly at him, and then cast them down.

'I have never cared for another woman since *that* time,' said the General after a pause ; 'and I never shall if I lived for—for—as long as the Brigade has been in Holland—and that is two hundred years.'

She laughed, but noiselessly; for she knew that when he began to talk thus, how his thoughts were wandering, and that he might, after all, begin to think that his future, for pleasure or pain, lay in the little white hands of the charming widow before him—of herself —the Mercedes of his early days by the Berbice river.

'As for the Count——' she began, but paused, for

the General made a gesture of impatience, and playing with his sword-knot, said :

'Well, you married him, and not John Kinloch. You are a free woman now; would you like to take my heart in your toils again, Mercedes, to make sport of it after all these years ?'

'Do not speak to me thus,' said she in her most seductive voice, as she touched his hand caressingly; 'I say too, after all these years, do not be so implacable. Ah! what must I think of you?'

'Think what you please.'

Again the long lashes flickered, and the snow-white eyelids drooped.

The General felt his position was becoming imperilled, that he 'was getting his flanks turned,' and so forth ; and he rose to retire.

But the General resumed his seat, and began to look a little vacantly and helplessly about him.

CHAPTER XI.

OMNIA VINCIT AMOR.

'IN the course of our lives it chances,' says a writer truly, 'that most of us influence directly or indirectly, in a greater or lesser degree, the lives of others ; but, as a general rule, we do not recognise this influence until *after* the effect has taken place.'

The Commandant of the Scots Brigade was yet to realise this.

There was a strange tremor in the usually stout heart of the general now, for though, after the sudden recognition of his first and, sooth to say, only love, he had begun to school himself to meet her with calmness or indifference, as a new friend, or old acquaintance, he felt himself as wax in her hands ; and that it was impossible, even after the lapse of all these years, to meet her unmoved, and to sit eye to eye, and listening to her voice—the voice that had thrilled his heart in the old time, and was thrilling it now again.

He took her hand in his, and she permitted him to retain it ; but for the life of him he knew not what to say, or how to take up the thread of the old story ; so she took the initiative.

' You were but a young lieutenant,' said she softly, ' when last we met.'

' And parted, as I said before.'

His reply conveyed a species of reproach, as he had much to forgive ; yet it seemed that there was an almost unconscious appeal in this reference to the old tie that bound them together once, and that *now*, did not seem to have been so completely severed after all.

'To my dying day, Mercedes, I thought I should remember your farewell glance at me,' said he.

'Forget it now,' she replied softly.

'Can I do otherwise?' he asked, as he read the shy light in downcast eyes. But oh, Mercedes, if—if——'

'What?' –

'But I must not think it now—if your sweet lips should be but tricking me again!'

'Oh, think not so!'

Round hers his hand closed once again, and with its clasp came the earnest of a promise that each would never fail the other again; and then a great brightness seemed suddenly to fall upon the hearts and lives of both.

'Oh face so loved in the past time!' said Kinloch, as he drew her towards him and kissed her fondly, to the growing amazement of Dolores, who was about to enter the room, but withdrew softly, her heart tremulous with joy, though laughing, as a young girl is sure to do, at what she deemed a pair of elderly lovers; and yet the General was barely in his fortieth year.

It seemed to her that his resentment against her

sex in general, and against widows in particular, had evaporated very quickly !

The General had felt the cold coquetry of Mercedes in the past—her desertion of him—too keenly, not to be deeply stirred and to feel her influence now.

The old love that in his heart had never died, but had been curiously woven up with a species of hate, came to the surface once more, and the assurance of it was flattering to the still beautiful Mercedes. 'Love,' it is said, 'cannot be measured by time ; it springs up like fungus in the night. It flourishes apace, and, like the wind, none know whence it cometh, or whither it goeth.'

'Could you care still for such a fogey as I have become ?' asked the General in a low voice ; 'care for me again, I mean ?'

'I am not now the thoughtless girl you loved in the past time.'

'But you are the woman I love now—the girl I never forgot and never ceased to love !' he exclaimed, while surprised at his own impetuosity and fluency. 'Once, at least, in our lives heaven seems to open to all of us : it opened to me when I first knew and loved Mercedes ; and now heaven seems to have come to me again !'

And now, to the memory of both, there came back

the murmur of the Berbice river, with its giant water-lilies ; the glorious moon and stars of the tropics, looking down on the grassy ramparts of Fort Nassau, the palisades and spires of New Amsterdam, and the love-scenes of the past time ; and when Kinloch rose to depart, it was with the promise that he would return betimes on the morrow.

It would be rather difficult to describe the emotions of the whilom misogynist, as he turned on his homeward way.

Joy at being restored to Mercedes, and gratified vanity that he could yet inspire love, conflicted curiously with a dread that he had compromised his own dignity and his long-vaunted opinions of the sex by this sudden surrender—this yielding to her great beauty and her old influence over him.

What would Drumlanrig, Dundas, and other old chums of the Brigade think of him? and what would Lewie Baronald say?—poor Lewie, whom he had doomed to foreign service to save him, as he had phrased it, 'from the fangs of Dolores'!

He felt his brown cheek blush hotly at the thought.

'That must be amended,' he muttered ; 'to-morrow I shall see the Director-General of Infantry.'

It was impossible for him to shut his eyes to the fact that Dolores was every way a desirable bride for

Lewic; and that, apart from her being the daughter of his own first and only love, she was the *lionne* of the Hague, who was fêted and courted, whose toilettes were copied, whose sallies were retailed, and who was the central figure in society there.

At last he stood in his old familiar room, where hung more than one old tattered colour of the Brigade, riven by Spanish bullets and Walloon pikes. How much had passed—how great was the change in his thoughts, hopes, and intentions, since he had left it, but a few hours ago!

He scarcely thought himself the same John Kinloch, as he drew forth the miniature from its secret drawer in the old cabinet, and sat down to contemplate it with loving and tender thoughts, and literally to ' feast ' his eyes, as the phrase is, on the face of her who, before she went to sleep that night, pressed her ripe coral lips to her own hand ; and they sought the exact place where the General, ere leaving, had pressed *his.*

CHAPTER XII.

CONCLUSION.

WE have not much more to relate.

Maurice Morganstjern quitted the Hague suddenly, and betook him on his diplomatic mission, whatever it was, to Paris; and his compatriot the Heer van Schrekhorn thought it conducive to his personal safety to make himself scarce about the same time; so both were beyond the just vengeance of Lewie Baronald.

Great was the amazement of the latter when he found his uncle, the General, quite *en famille* at the villa of the Countess, and learned from Dolores something of what had transpired on the night of the ridotto, and of her perilous adventure.

It seemed simply incredible!

'How now, uncle, about the name of Mercedes?' he asked him laughingly.

'What about it?' asked the General testily, yet reddening like a great schoolboy.

'Is it to go down in the annals of our family?'

'I hope so.'

'And how about all the Dead Sea fruit, the blackness of Gehenna, your firmness, and all that?'

'Silence, you young dog!'

And merrily laughed Dolores as she ran her white fingers over the piano, and sang a verse of the song that had now become so familiar to her :

> ' The love that I have chosen
>   Is to my heart's content ;
> The salt sea will be frozen,
>   Before that I repent.
> Repent it will I never,
>   Until the day I dee,
> Though the Lowlands o' Holland
>   Have parted my love and me.'

'And your home is Scotland—the home to which you may take me, is it like this?' asked the Countess softly of the General, as they sat in the recess of a window ; and from the question it may be safely gathered that events had progressed rapidly between them.

'Like *this !*' exclaimed the General ; 'you must see it for yourself to know the difference,' he added, as his eye swept the dull, dead flat of the Dutch landscape— flat as the flattest part of England.

Then he laughed as he thought of Thomincan over-shadowed by the majestic Ochills, the deep glens of which, with their solemn shadows and silence, are calculated to fill the soul at times with a species of poetic or melancholy ecstasy ; the grey precipices past which the river rushes to Loch Leven, and the old mansion on its rock—half chateau and half fortress—of which Mercedes would some day be chatelaine.

But soon after all this, a shock awaited the General, when an orderly dragoon placed in his hand a large official packet addressed to himself, and sealed with the official seal of the Dutch Republic.

It announced that which had long been expected, that their High Mightinesses the States-General had dispensed with the services of the Scots Brigade, and a day was named when it would embark on board a squadron of British ships for Scotland, and be placed, as so many of its officers now desired, at the disposal of his Britannic Majesty.

The General's heart gave a throb. He had ruthlessly been on the point of separating his nephew from Dolores ; and here, perhaps, he might eventually be separated from the old love he had so recently found again !

But Mercedes placed her hand in his, in token that they would never separate in life again.

So the old Brigade, of gallant memory, was going home *en masse* at last—home to Scotland, with its mighty crop of laurels, gathered in the Lowlands of

Holland, France, and Spain ; home after two hundred years of foreign service, during which, as the Scottish commander-in-chief soon after told its soldiers in Edinburgh, they had captured in battle and siege many a standard, but *never lost one.*

The brilliant sun of a July evening was shining on the broad blue waters of the Maese, and the pale-green willow groves that fringe its banks ; on the tossing sails of many a windmill far afield ; on the red mansions and spires of Rotterdam, the great brick tower of St. Laurence, and the high gables of the Hoeg Straat ; on the long line of the Boompjies with all their stately elms, when the old Scots Brigade, with the drums of all its battalions waking Dutch echoes for the last time to 'The Lowlands of Holland,' marched to the landing-place for embarkation, accompanied by vast crowds of sympathising, admiring, regretful, and kindly-hearted Dutch folk ; for a thousand old historical, warlike, and, better than all, friendly ties and associations were, on that evening, to be severed for ever !

Before that day of embarkation came, two marriages, which created the deepest interest in the departing Brigade (which the brides accompanied), had been celebrated at the Schotsche Kirk of the Hague, by its pastor, the Reverend Ichabod Crane : on which occasion there were present the Burgomaster; Heer van Otterbeck, the Minister of State ; and two or three of their Mightinesses of the States-General.

Need we say whose marriages these were ?

THE STORY

OF THE

CID RODRIGO OF BIVAR,

THE STORY OF THE CID RODRIGO OF BIVAR.

It is in old Castile, and on the banks of the rapid Ebro, that our story opens, during the wonderful era of the Cid Campeador, when in Spain there were about twenty kings, some of whom were Christians, but more were Mohammedans; and in the land were many independent warlike lords, who roved about on horseback, completely armed, with trains of knights, offering their services to princes and princesses who were at war.

This custom, says Voltaire, had already spread over Europe, but nowhere to such an extent as in Spain; the Christian knights were dubbed as such, with many solemn ceremonies, 'and watched their arms before the altar of the Virgin Mary; but the Moslem paladins were content with simply girding on a scimitar. This was the origin of knights-errant and of such numbers of single combats.'

What with twenty kings all warring among themselves; lawless robbers in the Sierras to fight; Jews to capture, torture, and mulct; knights-errant besetting the highways and bridges with shield uplifted to meet all comers ; Moors on every hand to slay without mercy, but more particularly at Seville, Granada, and Valencia, and the still more abhorred Morabathans, the restless spirits who wished to be up and doing, for good or for evil, amid the din of kettledrums and cymbals, the glitter of lances and banners and so forth, must have had plenty of work cut out for them in the sunny Spain of those days, long ere Cervantes had laughed her 'chivalry away.'

Near the right bank of the Ebro, about ten miles from Burgos, at the base of the Montanos de Santander, stood the Convent of Miraflores; and though many times repaired and renewed, it stands there still: but it was in the zenith of its fame when one day in the June of that year, while Sancho, the ambitious King of Castile, was preparing to besiege Zamora, an armed knight reined up his horse on its most sequestered side, where one solitary window overlooked the river and all the groves of olive and myrtle that grew thereby.

Though we write of a period so remote, strange to say the window is there still in the old wall, against

which the Moors have more than once hurled their
strength in vain, and it projects like a carved stone
cage of three pointed arches, supported by the head
and wings of a time-worn and gigantic figure of
grotesque design ; and thereat was a fair young face,
that grew bright with joy when the young knight drew
near.

The latter was a typical Spaniard, vigorous, tall, and
well developed in figure ; black haired, with eyes full
of fire ; dark, well-defined eyebrows, and features sharp
and grave. Save that he wore a species of Moorish
basinet, bright as silver, with a tippet of mail ; he was
clothed in chain armour to the tips of his fingers and
the soles of his feet, for the land teemed with fighting
and peril, and no man ventured abroad save completely equipped. His spurs were goads without
rowels, and a cross-hilted sword hung in his glittering
belt.

The girl who welcomed his approach was not a
religieuse, for young ladies were boarded in convents
then as now ; but her costume declared her to be of
rank, as it was of shiny, golden-yellow silk, trimmed
with black of the same material, tightly sleeved to the
wrist ; and she wore her thick, dark hair plaited in
several divisions, after the old Gothic custom that
lingered still in Spain.

Her complexion was fair and bright; her features delicate and harmonious; she was bewitching rather than beautiful—quite enough so to be the heroine even of a romance! and the *Madre Abadesa* of Miraflores, who had very special instructions given her regarding the care of this young lady, had accorded her the secluded apartment with the projecting window —a circumstance which led to the young knight discovering and making her acquaintance, a fact that would have filled the good lady with intense dismay— for by flirting their falcons, the young pair had come to a flirtation, and rather more, between themselves.

In those days he who bore the hawk on his left wrist in the most graceful way, was deemed the most accomplished cavalier; and to please ladies, it was the fashion to play flirty tricks with the pinions of their hawks. Thus, more than once, when passing, had the strange knight's hawk flown upward to the full length of its silken jess to flirt with the merlin on the hand of the lady, and hence it came to pass that the owners met as we find them. In those days people seem to have fallen in love more suddenly and desperately than they do in our railway times, and their love seemed always to delight in struggling with difficulties.

There was much of the Romeo and Juliet passionate

tenderness in the suddenly-developed regard of these
two, but we cannot suppose that the lovers of those
days spoke more 'on stilts' than those of the present
time. The old story that was first told in Eden will
have ever the tender trivialities and endearing epithets,
so we shall imagine all these said, and come to prose
at once.

'Your name, señor mio—dear love rather—in all
your visits you have never yet told it to me?' she
said softly.

'I have to win it yet,' he replied.

'Where?' she asked.

'Where does a hidalgo win his name save in battle
against the Moorish curs? When so won, you shall
know it. But yours, sweet lady?'

'May not, must not, be told to one who conceals
his own.'

'But I must call you something, Estrella mia,'
said he tenderly.

'Then your "star" be it,' said she, laughing and
kissing her hand to him, 'and my love and my prayers
go with you to battle.'

'Nay, I go not to battle just now.'

'Whither then, and armed thus?'

'To fulfil a vow of vengeance on a craven who smote
my aged father on the beard with his mailed hand.'

'Is it not better to forgive?'

'Some things, perhaps, but not a deed like that! Ay de mi, is it not hard for you to be shut up in this solitary place, dependent on yourself for all joy and amusement?'

'Nay, señor mio, I am content; and is not contentment joy? I shall never be happier than I am, till I rejoin my dear old father.'

'Where?' asked the knight.

'To tell that would be to disclose myself.'

'Tie a ribbon to my lance-head, thou dear one, and I shall dip it in the blood of him I have vowed to slay.'

She did so, saying in the spirit of the age:

'Rival, if you can, the Cid Rodrigo, who has been known to meet ten knights in arms, and unhorse them all; who, with his sword, slew that giant Moor, the Caliph of Cordova, and released six Christian maidens.'

The knight laughed lightly.

'Dios guarde à ustéd, mi querida!' he exclaimed, gathering up his reins, and spurring his horse—the Babieca of so many ballads and romances—for sooth to say, he was the identical Cid Rodrigo of whom she spoke; and waving a farewell to 'the sweet face at the window,' he rode off with lance and helmet flashing in the sun, and she watched him till he disappeared in the direction of Miranda—watched him departing on his deadly mission with less anxiety, perhaps, than a girl of the present day would see her lover start by express train.

The Convent of Miraflores, with its garden and vineyard, formed a kind of oasis in the long sweeping plain at the foot of the rugged Sierra ; shy bustards stalked about there in the loneliness amid the silent scenery, for silent it is in Spain, where there are no singing birds. A train of mules crossing the waste, where the wild mignonette grows still in sheets of green ; a solitary horseman in mail, with lance-head glittering in the sun, or a friar jogging along on a mule, alone were seen from time to time from the convent windows.

Gentle and soft in disposition, the fair *pensionaria* had a deal of pent-up tenderness at her disposal. Hitherto it had been bestowed upon pet birds and flowers, mingled with many prayers in chapel and much musing and reverie at the projecting window, where she would sit for hours in that non-literary age, when there were no books, no Berlin wool-work, and no pianos, gazing at the sparkling stars of the summer night or at the morning sun, as he tipped the transparent foliage of the myrtle groves and lit up the current of the Ebro ; till a day came when she was

roused and excited by finding a gallant hawk, hooded
and plumed, flirting with the merlin on her wrist, and
saw its owner, the young mailed horseman, below the
window regarding her with pleasure and admiration ;
and as he had some trouble in luring back his bird, a
secret acquaintance, that ripened into love, began
between these two.   The girl—for she was but a girl,
and very young too—loved with all her newly-
awakened woman's heart and with a wild yearning,
very different, perhaps, from that of a young woman
of the present day, for her life was one of intense
seclusion, and he rapidly became (like Romeo) 'the
god of her idolatry' in the unreasoning enthusiasm of
those days of romance and chivalry.

How little could she dream that her lover was the
Cid Rodrigo of Bivar, with the fame of whose
exploits all Spain resounded now !

He was born at Burgos, where his father, Don
Diego Lainez, was a powerful noble, and his mother
was Donna Teresa, 'daughter of the Conde Don Nuno
Alvarez,' as the inscription on her tomb bears now in
the church of San Pedro de Cordova, near Burgos.

In the year our story opens, the aged Don Diego
had been grossly insulted by the haughty and powerful
Count of Gormaz, better known as Don Lozano
Gomez, who dared, with his iron gauntlet, to smite

him on the face in presence of Sancho the King and
his Court. Mingled fury and deep dejection filled the
heart of the old man at this unparalleled affront; he
refused food; sleep left his eyelids, and hourly he
brooded on his dire disgrace, till his son Rodrigo
vowed to avenge him. Before the miraculous crucifix
which is still in the Cathedral of Burgos, and which
tradition avers to have been fashioned by St. Nicodemus,
he had sworn to do this—and so strongly were the
minds of men constituted in those days, that even as
he registered the evil vow, his heart was filled by a
glow of reverence and adoration—and then he rode
forth in search of their enemy, for these were not times
like our own, when young fellows affect to be so much
'used up' in all the joys and sorrows of the world that
nothing excites them.

Quitting the vicinity of the Convent of Miraflores, he
took the way to Miranda del Ebro, and had not ridden
many miles when he saw an armed knight approaching, attended by four esquires, or men-at-arms, and a
sense of fierce joy filled the soul of the Cid on recog-
nising, by the blazoning of his surcoat, the very man of
whom he was in search, Don Lozano, the Conde de
Gormaz, delivered over to him, as he believed, specially
by the hand of Heaven! Goldsmith tells us that 'it
is easier to conceive than describe the complicated

sensations which are felt from the pain of a recent
injury and the pleasure of approaching vengeance;'
and some such mingled emotion there was in the
heart of the knight.

Reining up his horse in the centre of the narrow and
dusty road, Rodrigo cried :

'Don Lozano—craven dog, who smote my father,
defend yourself!'

'Begone, rash youth, lest I have you disarmed and
scourged!' replied Lozano, lowering his lance however,
as he knew that he who barred the way would not
stand on trifles. 'We are five to one.'

'Villain, come on ! on my side are right and nobility
—worth a hundred comrades!' cried Rodrigo ; and
meeting at full speed with a dreadful shock, the
splinters of their lances flew twenty feet into the air.
Rodrigo then drew his sword, the famous Tisona, and
almost ere Lozano's blade had left its sheath, he was
hewn down from his saddle and bleeding in the dust,
while his armed attendants in terror took to flight.
Rodrigo then tore the surcoat from the dying Count,
as a token of his victory—Mariana the historian, we
think, adds that he cut off his head—and then rode
leisurely homeward to Burgos ; for if a little homicide
by way of duello was thought little of here when
George III. was King, it was a matter of decidedly

less consequence in Spain in the days of the Cid.

At the head of three hundred mounted hidalgos, 'all wearing gold and silken raiment, with perfumed gloves, and caps of gorgeous colours,' Don Diego, now, as he thought, redeemed from disgrace, rode forth to meet the King and kiss his hand, while Rodrigo repaired to the Convent of Miraflores, with the blood-stained ribbon streaming from his casque, but the face was not at the window now. Thrice he came thither and watched and waited for it in vain, and believing that the Mother Abbess had discovered his love-affair, he returned with a heavy heart to Burgos, to take counsel of the King Sancho, though some say it was of this latter's father, King Ferdinand.

But soon tidings came to the Court of Castile that a beautiful lady, who had been foully wronged, was coming hither attended by a numerous train, to seek justice at the hands of the King. All the young knights were ready to embrace her cause, whatever it might be; but all, including the famous Bellido Dolfos, withdrew in favour of Rodrigo, who first demanded to make it his own; and yet he thought, 'God wot, why should I champion her, when my own and only love is the Recluse of Miraflores?' And then the sweet face at the window came before him in memory with all the soft brightness of an opium-eater's dream.

Clad in black, with a gauze veil over her dark dishevelled tresses, her eyes streaming with tears, the lady fell on her knees before the King, exclaiming, as the Spanish ballad has it :

> 'Justice, King ! I am for justice—
> Vengeance on a traitor knight !
> Grant it me !   So shall thy children
> Thrive and prove thy soul's delight.'

Her voice found a painful echo in the heart of Rodrigo, who was filled with sudden horror.

'Estrella mia !' he exclaimed, as she threw up her veil ; 'can such sorrow be ? Are you Ximena Gomez?'

'And *you*—you—the slayer of my hapless father ! O mi padre murio !' she cried in a piercing voice, as they both made this terrible discovery.   Filial affection had been a ruling passion in the gentle mind of Ximena, who now experienced a dreadful shock on finding that it was by the hand of her lover, her father had perished.   And great too was the grief and dismay of the young Cid at a catastrophe—a revelation so unexpected.   A blight fell upon the hearts of both. Lozano had no son to avenge his death.   He left only the helpless and weeping Ximena, whom the King raised up, and who now ceased to demand on Rodrigo

the punishment she had craved before, and returned
to Miraflores, vowing that she would take the veil,
while Rodrigo, accompanied by his comrades, Bellido
Dolfos, Pedro Bermudez, and Martin Pelaez, Ordono,
and others, plunged at once into a series of warlike
exploits and expeditions, seeking to appease thereby
the memory of the sorrow that had fallen upon them
all. 'Of all the knights, the Cid distinguished himself
most against the Mussulmans,' says Voltaire briefly.
'Many of them ranged themselves under his banner,
and altogether, with their squires and horsemen in
armour, composed an army covered with iron and
mounted on the finest horses in the country. The
Cid conquered more than one Moorish king, and
having at last fortified himself in the city of Alcazar,
formed there a little sovereignty.'

Spanish history makes the conquered kings five in
number, and states that he caused them to pay tribute
after he set them at liberty, 'wherefore they served him
faithfully, and called him their Cid, or Lord.' It also
records that Ximena did not take the veil at Miraflores, but, curiously enough, exhibited another strange
sample of the manners of the age by petitioning the
King 'either to execute Rodrigo for killing her father,
or give him to her for a husband. The King chose
the latter, and Rodrigo joyfully received Ximena and

took her to his mother, who kept her as her own child, and they were betrothed; but Rodrigo promised to gain many more battles against the Moors before he would claim her as his wife.' And so, while the Cid was winning five provinces, and gaining glory too, with the edge of Tisona among the infidels—of whom he slew an incredible number, till a saying of his is a Spanish proverb to this day, 'The more Moors the more gain'—Ximena spent her time in fear and hope among her favourite flowers and love-birds at the house of Donna Teresa, in Burgos (Coronico de los Moros, etc.).

And even after their marriage it was his boast, 'God wot! oftener is Tisona than Ximena by my side.'

After the siege of Zamora, during which King Sancho was slain—treacherously, it is averred, by Don Bellido Dolfos—the Cid, as the former was repairing to Burgos, gave him a special message to Ximena:

'Tell her that I am coming; and, as an earnest thereof, give her this ring, which I took from the hand of the Caliph of Cordova.'

Don Billido, who in his heart cherished a secret and treacherous love for the betrothed of his friend, took the ring, and, saying emphatically, 'Rodrigo, amigo mio, haya cuenta sobre mi' (*i.e.*, 'My friend, rely on me'), rode gaily home to Burgos.

Bellido has been described as a man with a fierce hooked nose, a black beard, and slightly treacherous eyes, that, if such are the true index of the soul, might have revealed his natural character.

He gave the ring to Ximena, and told her that the Cid awaited her at Miraflores. She was surprised at this, but, never doubting the comrade of her intended husband, attended by two ladies, she set out for Mira-flores, closely veiled. They rode white palfreys, with velvet caparisons embroidered with gold, and having silken bridles covered with little bells. Bellido and some ruffians, on whom he could rely, formed their escort; but they never reached Miraflores.

In due time the Cid Rodrigo came to Burgos with his heart full of Ximena, his old love for her mingling with gratitude that she had forgiven him for the terrible wrong he had done her, and already he seemed to see her winning smile and her soft and lustrous eyes, that looked so truthfully under the long, dark lashes that fringed them.

'Madre mia, where is Ximena?' he exclaimed, as he alighted from his horse.

'At Miraflores, whither you sent for her,' was the reply.

'I sent no such message—there is some mistake.'

'Or treachery,' said Donna Teresa; 'my mind misgives me, or I distrust Don Bellido.'

'Can he have decoyed her away!' exclaimed the Cid, with alarm and rage in his voice and eye.

But the old lady knew not what to think, and began to weep bitterly; and still more did she weep when sure tidings came that in revenge for repelling his addresses, the double traitor Bellido Dolfos had betrayed Ximena into the hands of Hiaja, the savage Caliph of Toledo.

Rodrigo was beside himself with sorrow and dismay; but bethought him at once of his sword, and prevailed upon his new master, Alphonso VI., King of Old Castile, to besiege the city of Toledo, offering him all his knights for that enterprise.

The report of this siege, and the cause thereof—a Christian lady of rare beauty and high rank, more than all, the betrothed of the Cid, being a captive in the hands of the odious Hiaja—brought many knights and princes from distant lands, particularly Raymond, Count of Toulouse, and two princes of the royal blood of France, of the branch of Burgundy.

Their armies covered all the fertile plain amid which Toledo stands, on a steep hill, round the base of which flows the Tagus. In some places the spears of

the infantry—whose massed columns seemed like a
sea of glittering steel—stood thick as upright corn ;
in others were the squadrons of barbed horse, the
knights and men-at-arms, all clothed in chain armour,
bright as winter frost or polished silver, their many-
coloured plumes, their square banners, and swallow-
tailed pennons streaming out upon the wind.

High over all, with its towers and the minarets of its
mosques, rose the then infidel city of Toledo, the upper
part of which was then, as now, girt by Roman, and
the lower part by Moorish walls.   History tells us
that when Alphonso VI. had been a fugitive under
the persecution of his brother and predecessor, Sancho,
he had found an asylum at the Court of the Caliph of
Toledo, who treated him with hospitality and princely
distinction ; and now more than one Moorish warrior
rode forth from the city to reproach Alphonso with
ingratitude to his benefactor, and many a terrible and
remarkable combat was fought under the walls of
Toledo, among the defenders of which was Don Bellido
Dolfos, who had renounced his faith and adopted the
turban.

In the combats before the city, the Cid was daily
occupied, and many a Moorish warrior, horse and
man, rolled in the dust beneath his lance or battle-
axe ; and his followers were enriched by the spoil, the

rare weapons, the costly garments and jewels, that his hand won.

At last there came a day—the anniversary of the victory won by Mohammed at Bedr, between Mecca and Medina—when the Moors made a dreadful sortie from Toledo, led by the renegade, Bellido Dolfos ; and closing in on every hand, the Christians met them with equal ardour and fury.

The hand-to-hand fighting was terrible, and the Christian knights, led by the Cid, the Count of Toulouse, and others, dashed their horses through and through the living tide of Moors that surged around them.   Gorgeous as a field of flowers, with their many-coloured turbans and flowing garments, seemed the Moors as they kept shoulder to shoulder, guarding their heads with round shields covered with glittering bosses, their sharp scimitars flashing in the sun, their shouts rolling like thunder between the Tagus and the walls of Toledo, as they fought with demoniac strength and ferocity, but fought in vain.   High over all the throng towered the Cid upon Babieca, its mailed flanks stuck full of arrows and even broken lances.

'Santiágo y cerra España!' he shouted ever and anon—the old war-cry of Spain—and he hewed on all sides with Tisona, till his sword-arm grew weary, and the last who bit the dust beneath it was the traitor

Don Bellido, after whose fall the Moors were driven headlong into Toledo.

The siege lasted a year, during which Ximena and her two attendants occupied a noble chamber in the palace of the Caliph. Its ceiling was adorned with arabesques and fretwork, brilliant with gold and delicate pencilling. In its centre was an alabaster fountain of perfumed water, and round it were cages of gold and silver wire, full of singing birds ; and there daily the three ladies offered up their prayers on their knees for the success of the Christian arms, and for their own release.

After a year and a day Toledo capitulated, and Ximena was restored to the Cid, to whom all New Castile submitted, and who took possession of it in the name of Alphonso VI. ; and Madrid, then a small village, one day to become the capital of Spain, was for the first time in the hands of the Christians, and Hiaja was the last Caliph of Toledo.

To narrate all the heroic deeds performed by the Cid after his marriage would require the space of a very large volume indeed. The great dominions he acquired for his royal master the latter increased by espousing Zaid, a daughter of the Moorish King of Andalusia, after which Rodrigo, at the head of his knights, subdued the whole of Valentia. No sovereign

prince in Spain was more powerful than he ; but he
contented himself with the title of Cid, and never
assumed that of King, though he might easily have
done so. No warrior in Spain did more evil to the
Moors, yet he occasionally joined the Beni Huds of
Zaragossa against the Counts of Barcelona, whom he
conquered twice. While he never failed in his word
to a Christian, he mercilessly despoiled the Jews, from
two of whom he raised money for war, by depositing
with them two chests which were alleged to be full of
plate, but which contained only stones and sand.

His two daughters became queens of Aragon and
Navarre.

Five years after the conquest of Valentia, worn out
by incessant warfare, he fell ill, and was abed when
tidings were brought to him that Bucar, the Moor,
whom he had expelled from that kingdom, was
advancing to regain it with a mighty army of horse
and foot ; but Tisona lay idly in the scabbard now.
For seven days preceding his death, the Cid would
taste nothing but a little myrrh and balsam ; and on
the day he departed he took a solemn farewell of
Ximena, his kinsmen, and all his knights, whom he
requested to carefully bury his old war-horse Babieca,
' to the end that no dogs might eat the flesh of him
whose hoofs had trodden down so much dog's-flesh of

the Moors.' He bequeathed a coffer of silver to the two Jews, and desired that his body should be borne to San Pedro de Cardena, and laid beside that of his mother.

He died in the year 1097 ; but he who had been the terror of the Moors for so many years when in life, was still fated to strike terror to them in death, even while all the host of King Bucar were rejoicing that he had passed away. At midnight, twelve days after that event, the Christians prepared to abandon the city of Valentia—'Valentia of the Cid,' as it is called to this day. His body, which had been placed, we are told, ' in a sitting posture, and left to stiffen between two boards,' was placed on the back of Babieca, upright in the saddle, with the feet tied in the stirrups. To all appearance he was completely armed ; a light shield of parchment, painted with his device, was hung on his left arm ; the terrible Tisona was fixed bare and upright in his sword-hand. Geronymo, Bishop of Valentia, led Babieca by the rein ; Pedro Bermudez, with the banner of the Cid upraised, led the van with 400 knights ; then came the Cid's body, with Ximena and her ladies, guarded by 600 men, and when day broke, though the Moors were terrified to find that the Cid was there in his saddle again, a battle ensued, and King Bucar was defeated ; but Valentia was lost, and the sorrowing warriors of Rodrigo continued their retreat to Old Castile and beyond the Ebro.

At Olmedo they were met by his daughters, with all the knights of Aragon, clad in black cloaks, with hoods rent, and their shields reversed at their saddle bows ; and with every religious and military solemnity incident to the time, they laid him in his grave at San Pedro de Cardena, and two years afterwards Gil Diaz, one of his most faithful followers, buried Babieca before the gate of the church there. In the course of seven centuries and a half the remains of the famous Cid Rodrigo have been removed several times, the last occasion being by the French, in 1809, to the Espolen, or public promenade of Burgos ; but in 1826 they were restored to San Pedro, where the tomb and effigies of himself and Ximena now remain in a small but noble chapel. In that chapel lie the bones of · Alvar Fanez Minaya, whom he was wont to call his 'right arm ;' of Pedro Bermudez, Ordono, Martin Pelaez, the Asturian, and many more of his captains and valiant friends.

His statue, as ' the dread and terror of the Moorish curs,' has a prominent place in the quaint gateway of Santa Maria, erected by Charles V. at Burgos. In the time of Cervantes the saddle of Babieca was preserved in the Royal Armoury at Madrid, and Southey avers that he had personally seen and handled Tisona, now an heirloom in the family of the Marquis de Falces. On one side of the blade is graven, ' I am Tisona, made in the year 1002 ;' on the other is the legend, 'AVE MARIA GRATIA PLENA DOMINUS TUUM.'

THE BOY-GENERAL.

THE STORY OF JEAN CAVALIER.

THE BOY-GENERAL.

THE STORY OF JEAN CAVALIER.

'GUILLOT—you here! Why have you left the mountain of St. Julian?'

'To be with you, brother Jean—to fight for the Cevennes.'

'With a beardless face and a feeble hand!'

'I have about as much beard as you, mon frère; and if my hand be feeble, it has brought down many a wolf in Mialet and the Gevaudan,' replied Guillot, slapping the butt of his carbine emphatically.

The speakers were young Guillot Cavalier and his elder brother Jean, who was then, at the age of *seventeen years*, actually a general and second in command of the Camisard army, the Insurgent Protestants of Languedoc; who fought many a battle with Villars and De Montrevel, the best leaders of the age; who, with Roland, led the great revolt in 1703; and who

in his twentieth year became a full colonel in the
English army !

Both were very handsome lads, and both wore the
white tunic (in Languedocian, *camisa*) to distinguish
themselves from their enemies, and hence their well-
known name of Camisards. Both were well armed,
with swords, silver-mounted pistols, and short car-
bines ; but the elder wore over his shoulder the scarf
of a French general, and in his white velvet cap the
wing of an eagle. Strong—and tender as strong—
was the bond of affection between these two lads, who
had both been born in the village of Ribaute, among
the pastoral mountains north of the Valley of Gardon ;
and though Jean was ready to face any peril and to
' do all that may become a man ' for the cause in
which he had been so suddenly made a leader, and in
which he had already won such high distinction, his
heart sank at the contemplation of Guillot—a delicate
boy, and their mother's chief care—encountering the
risks of that most savage and rancorous Civil War
which now devastated Languedoc.

Jean, as a very little boy, had been bred a shepherd,
and was afterwards apprenticed to a baker at Anduze ;
and it was from the employ of the latter that, with
a carbine in his hand, he went forth to become a
Camisard, ' and soon proved himself to be,' as history

tells us, 'a most able general, as well as a powerful prophet and preacher.'

'Return, Guillot—return,' he is said to have urged again ; ' our poor mother cannot spare us both.'

' La Bonne Madelon is the mother we must serve just now, and I will not quit your camp,' replied Guillot, whose eyes lit up, as he referred to one of those wild, half-frenzied, and wholly enthusiastic prophetesses, or female preachers, who thronged the camps of the Camisards, attended their councils, and followed them into battle.

' Then be it so,' said Jean Cavalier resignedly ; adding, ' I have good news for you and all the faithful, Guillot. The Queen of Great Britain—the good Queen Anne—is sending a fleet to our aid.'

' Of what use will it be to us among the mountains ?' asked Guillot, laughing.

' It brings us troops, Guillot—troops, who will help us to beat those of Montrevel,' replied Jean, referring to the expedition consisting of thirty-five British and twelve Dutch ships of the line, which was to sail on the 1st of July, 1703, from St. Helens, to the assistance of the Cevennois, and to the arrival of this expedition off the coast the elder Cavalier looked confidently forward to repulsing the column of De Montrevel, while Roland was fighting the King's troops elsewhere. And now to explain briefly what brought all these affairs about.

In the 'Histoire des Pasteurs du Désert,' and other annals, we are told the terrible story of that Civil War in which 30,000 Cevennols perished in battle or on the scaffold, between November, 1702, and December, 1704. Well fitted for desultory warfare are the mountains of Cevennes, with their rocky labyrinth of deep gorges and dark defiles, which a mere. handful of bold peasantry were able to hold against the best troops of Louis XIV., and where, to this hour, the population is almost entirely Protestant, inhabiting some six hundred villages, which are all but inaccessible.

The white-shirted Camisards had these steep ridges to encamp on ; gorges for ambuscades ; forests to rally in ; paths trodden only by the wolf or the fox to retreat by ; and caverns which became their arsenals and fortresses. Army after army came to annihilate these peasants as heretics, after the Revocation of the Edict of Nantes, but only to be destroyed or hurled in ruin and defeat into the valleys ; but the miseries of the war, the slaughter of women and children, the burning and pillaging were fearful, and spread from thence to the ocean on the south, and the Rhone on the east, among the hundred churches of Dauphine.

With much sublime piety and heroic valour the armed peasantry, as in the similar case of the Scottish Covenanters, combined a great amount of psalm-singing and the strongest religious fervour, bordering at times upon fanaticism, and prophets and prophetesses, like La Bonne Madelon, roused a wildness of enthusiasm never seen in France since the days of Joan of Arc. ' The spirit of resistance began to show itself, drawn forth by the recital of their wrongs, the denunciation of their tyrants, and the assurance of support from heaven ; conventicles were held, in spite of the terrors of prison, torture, and the soldiery, and in the open air among the rocks and caverns.'

Roland and Cavalier levied their troops from the different parishes, each of which furnished its quota of armed men and money, and fresh heroes to fill up the vacancies in the ranks. Many believed themselves to be sword or bullet proof, while ' the seizures, tortures, executions by breaking on the wheel and burning alive (the common modes of punishing a Camisard), led to reprisals on their part—to the slaying of priests and the sacking and burning of Catholic churches.' But in the spirit of outrage, the French troops were far surpassed by the guerilla bands, called Florentins, in the pay of the Grand Monarque.

Jean Cavalier thought of these things keenly now,

as he gazed on the soft boyish face of his brother
Guillot, when posting his column of Camisards in
ambush one morning, ere dawn, to give a hot welcome
to the royal forces under the Sieur de Montrevel, an
officer high in repute for great valour, but merciless in
his severity.

The sound of the drums had died away, but the
sheeny bayonets glistened in the sun, and the white
Bourbon colours of the regiments, with their golden
fleur-de-lys, were waving in the wind, as the column
of royal troops began to penetrate a defile that was
clothed with the olive, the vine, and the fig-tree.
The church and hamlet there had perished by fire ;
the place was desolate ; not a human being was
visible, and without halting, the troops pushed on,
with an advanced guard to 'feel the way,' in front,
till they reached a portion of the defile where the
impending rocks were higher, the way narrower, and
the trailing vines had given place to the dense, dark,
and woody luxuriance of forest trees. The flower of
the column was composed of one of the four battalions of the ancient regiment of Champagne, raised
so far back as the reign of Henry II.

'Halt!' cried the officer of the advanced guard,
whose quick eye had detected the bright flash of steel
amid the green branches. In another moment, a

combination of fearful sounds burst like a storm upon the silent air, while the soldiers halted, panting with the exertion of climbing the long and steep ascent. An enormous fragment of rock, dislodged from above, crashed with the sound of thunder into the defile below, a mass that must have annihilated the entire advanced guard, had the officer not halted it in time. Other masses of rock and rubbish came thundering down, barring all advance, while more than a thousand voices made the defile re-echo with the shouts of fierce exultation, mingled with a religious hymn.

On the fallen rock in front there was suddenly seen a female, ' the Good Madelon,' kneeling in an attitude of frenzied supplication, her arms thrown wildly up, her hands clasped, her black hair floating loose, her drapery streaming on the wind, and by her side stood Cavalier. As yet no shots had been fired.

' Voilà! 'Tis the rebel Cavalier!' cried De Montrevel, almost leaping in his saddle with exultation ; and his sharp words of command followed fast.

A volley was poured in front and on both flanks, and from these three points it was closely responded to ; and then the soldiers, who were in great force, began, at the bayonet's point, to push up the woody sides of the defile, firing as they went and driving the

peasantry before them ; and meanwhile the prophetess
—she of the supposed charmed life, La Bonne Madelon,
remained on her knees immovable, absorbed in prayer,
half seen, half hidden, amid the eddying smoke.
Guillot strove to lead her aside, but in vain ; and when
a bullet grazed his cheek, he rushed away to join his
brother, who, like him, strongly believed in the power
of immunity from death possessed by Madelon, and
was now busy in the act of concentrating and direct-
ing the operations of his scattered followers.

It is said that when the prophetess, whose eyes had
in them the gleam of insanity, felt the bullets whiz
about her, a sense of danger came with the sound, and
that she opened her eyes and glanced about her, as if
seeking to escape, but she was grasped by four
soldiers of the line ; and that when the Camisards
beheld her feeble hands bound with cords, while her
head sunk on her breast, and she was dragged away,
they became for a time panic-stricken, and though
they hovered on the precipice above the corpse-
strewn defile, they ceased to fire, and gazed on her
conveyance to the rear in a species of stupid
wonder.

'She can save herself,' Cavalier is reported to have
said, so perfect was his belief, as a credulous moun-
taineer, in her divine mission ; 'we cannot rescue her

now, but,' he added, lifting his cap and looking upward, 'some miracle from heaven will.'

But no miracle was wrought, and with his solitary prisoner the Sieur de Montrevel marched down, somewhat triumphantly, to the nearest town, the white houses of which could be seen a league or two distant from the mountains. That night Guillot, with a chosen party, stole from them, and entered the silent street, from which all the inhabitants had fled, hoping to find some trace of the Good Madelon, perhaps in the public prison, from which they might see a way to free her.

But Montrevel and his men had departed, leaving in the market-place a fearful object, which greeted the eyes of Guillot and his followers when daybreak came in. Suspended by the neck from a gibbet in the centre of the place hung the body of their prophetess in its well-known drapery, and literally full of bullets, as the departing Florentins had made a target of it. She had been a beautiful woman, whose husband and children had been cruelly destroyed before her, and sorrow had doubtless turned her brain.

Accustomed though they had become to atrocities, the Camisards gazed at each other in horror at this spectacle, and then bore away her body for interment, sadly, slowly, and reverentially, and from the side of her grave went up the united vow for vengeance!

10

The fleet of Sir Cloudesley Shovel failed to land either succour or allies, and returning to England, says Schomberg, in his 'Naval Chronology,' was off the Isle of Wight on the 16th of November; so the Camisards now had no hopes but in their own hearts and hands.

Intent on avenging the barbarous death of the Good Madelon, Jean Cavalier, with 1,500 Camisards, took post near La Tour de Bellot, a deserted sheep-farm and watch-tower to the westward of Alais, from whence he meant to issue and attack De Montrevel, who was, he believed, ignorant of his vicinity, and who, keeping somewhat careless guard, was encamped not far off among the mountains. In the afternoon the Camisards were plentifully supplied with food by a wealthy miller on the Gardon, whom they believed to be true to their cause. By nightfall, Cavalier had reconnoitred all the country; and as the sun set, dark clouds gathered fast, and premature twilight shrouded the valleys. Through them the wind howled, fore-boding a storm, and Cavalier laughed with stern joy, when telling his followers that their attack would be veiled by the war of the elements.

He had laid out his plans with wisdom, and alone, and a little apart from his troops, was waiting the time to give them the signal to move, when from all

points around the Tour de Bellot burst forth a half-
random storm of musketry, and the boom of cannon
announced that the King's troops were upon him!

'We are betrayed!' cried Guillot, rushing bareheaded to his side.

'By whom?'

'The miller of the Gardon!' replied Guillot, passionately.

And so it was; ere the Camisard outposts had been
able to give the alarm, they were cut to pieces, and
only Cavalier and a few of his men were able to sally
from the tower before it was invested on all sides.
Guillot and others were shut up in it! Furious were
the efforts made by Cavalier—efforts urged by filial
love and despair—to drive back the soldiers and
relieve those in the tower, from the windows and
every cranny of which its slender garrison poured a
deadly fire for eight hours, till their ammunition was
expended, and then the edifice was set on fire; 290
perished in it, says history, 100 Camisards lay dead
outside, and around it were 1,200 of the King's troops
killed or wounded!

Compelled to retire some distance, yet fighting every
inch of the way, Cavalier beheld, with horror, the
tower sheeted with fire. His soul died within him as
he thought of his brother, the boyish and gentle

Guillot, and all who were perishing there, and he strove to fight his way back just as day was breaking, and by the light of it he could see, apart from all the hurly-burly of the strife, a remarkable combat proceeding, and on the very verge of a cliff close by.

It was a boy—a boy, sword in hand—Guillot, fighting with a young officer of the Regiment of Champagne. His cap was off—his white camisa was stained by blood and dirt and scorched with fire. Borne back by bayonets, Cavalier could only look on in agony, as he saw his brother driven step by step to the very verge of the dreadful cliff behind him, and of which he was unaware. Unyielding, though retreating, Guillot kept parrying thrusts and warding cuts with consummate skill, till a cry escaped him, and he vanished!

A groan from the breast of Cavalier echoed that cry; a mist came over his sight, yet he continued to fight, like a blind man, to cover the retreat of the wreck of his followers, by whom wild justice was soon after done on the treacherous miller. He was seized, condemned to death, and led out to execution in front of the insurgents, who, according to their wont, knelt around him, while offering up prayers for his soul. His parting embrace was refused by his two sons, who served under Cavalier, and who looked on unmoved by the terrible death he had to die.

That his brother Guillot might perish in battle, or by torture in the hands of the enemy, Cavalier had always dreaded ; but the catastrophe by which he lost him was altogether unconceived : and the fortunes of the conflict led him far from the vicinity of La Tour de Bellot, thus he could neither search for the remains of Guillot, nor bestow funeral rites upon them.

For months the war went on. The bright valour and cool judgment of Cavalier, ' the Boy-General,' for such he was, exalted him still more above all other leaders of the Camisards, and especially so when he succeeded in utterly defeating a considerable body of the royal troops at Martinarque, under the Sieur de Montrevel, who commanded them.

The 6th of April, 1704, saw Cavalier again betrayed by one he trusted. At the head of 900 foot and 300 horse, all well equipped, he entered the Vaunage, or Valley of Noyes, so called from a little town of that name, in the fertile district westward of Nismes, intending to waylay the Maréchal de Montrevel, who was on the way to Montpellier, but was himself lured into a dreadful ambuscade, and surrounded on all sides by the royal troops, including a great body of King James's · Irish, who had recently fought at the battle of the Boyne.

On all sides burst forth from amid the shelter of

trees and hedgerows the withering fire of musketry, the boom of the cannon, and the hissing showers of grape.

Undismayed by the sudden scene of carnage, and by numbers six times exceeding his own, Cavalier, perceiving a design of the enemy to completely cut him off, 'wheeled his column rapidly round under the hottest fire, and in the face of a charge of bayonets drew off his men, retreating in échelon—a masterly manœuvre of the baker's boy, which drew forth the admiration of the Maréchal Duc de Villars.'

Eventually, however, his retreat was cut off, the royal troops occupied every height, every avenue and pass that remained, and nothing was left for him now but to cut his way out at all hazards, or die! He was not long in choosing. 'Throwing aside his magnificent uniform and white plume, he put on a common dress,' we are told, and ordering his comrades to close their ranks, made a headlong dash at the enemy.

'Notre Dame de frappe morte!' was the shout of the regiments of Champagne and Normandy, as they brought their bayonets to the charge; but Cavalier broke through the first line. In the attack on the second, he was singled out when discovered, and a soldier seized the bridle of his horse, but had his hand hewn off by a young Camisard wearing a scarlet scarf

over his white camisa. He was next grasped by a
dragoon, whom he pistolled ; but now, beyond appeared another line and a whole squadron of dragoons
barring his way to the Pont de Rosni—the only issue.
Panic-struck, his fugitive horsemen poured madly
down upon it sword in hand, forgetful for a time of
their leader, who was in the rear, and who would
probably have been cut off but for the young Camisard
in the red scarf—his brother—his brother Guillot (of
whose escape anon), who suddenly appeared upon the
ground—'his brother, a boy *ten* (?) years old,' says the
French account, 'who drew his horse across the
bridge, and with a pistol presented to the fugitives,
summoned them to defend their chief and not abandon
him.'

Cavalier, with the remainder of his force, escaped
into the forest of Cannes. This battle extended over
all the ground from the mill of Langlode to the town
of Noyes. Of one thousand dead who lay on the field,
one half were Camisards. During the whole of the
conflict one of their prophets, named Daniel Gui, stood
on the summit of a rock, amid six female enthusiasts,
three of whom were afterwards shot, invoking the God
of Battles to favour their cause.

The miraculous restoration of his brother—for such
it was deemed—alone was a palliation to the heart of

Cavalier for the deep mortification of his defeat; and yet it had come about simply enough. Recent rains had formed a deep basin of water under the cliff from which he fell, in a place where jagged rocks alone had been visible shortly before. Sinking, he rose to the surface, struggled to the bank, faint and wounded, and had found shelder, till well and whole, in a shepherd's hut, till he could join his brother in the Valley of the Noyes, and now tender indeed was their meeting and the mutual embrace they gave each other.

But brief time had they for mutual explanations, as ere long the report of musketry began to wake the echoes of the forest, and Daniel Gui came rushing in with tidings that the Sieur de Lalande was putting to the sword the entire inhabitants of the village of Euzet. Entering it suddenly, he had found a bullock newly-skinned, and bales of hams, bread, and sausages made up for the men of Cavalier, whom he at once traced and attacked with vigour, and defeated with the loss of 170 men. Final vengeance now fell on the unhappy villagers of Euzet, which, together with a cavern close by, was found to be full of the wounded, ammunition, medicine, and stores of Cavalier's forces. This sealed the fate of the former; and every human being lying there was slaughtered, including the helpless creatures in the cavern. Such was the awful system on which this war was carried on.

Cavalier's commissariat was supplied by requisitions upon districts, irrespective of their faith, and when not given with goodwill, he was compelled to write thus to the chief magistrate of the place :

'MM.,—Vous ne manquerez point de nous préparer demain le diner, son peine d'être assiégé et mis *à feu et à sang !*—CAVALIER.'

But it was while he was still struggling manfully and bravely to maintain a desperate cause against the whole force of the French army that the crushing intelligence came to him of the fall of his compatriot, Roland Laporte. This was on the 13th of August, 1704, at Castelnau, near the Ners, a river which in winter rolls down from the mountains in a mighty flood.

His presence there would seem to have been betrayed to the Duc de Villars. At midnight, when he and his companions were fast asleep, the sentinel on the tower-head suddenly heard amid the stillness of the hour the distant noise of horses approaching at a furious gallop, and gave the alarm just as a column of cavalry was entering the town.

Half-clad and half-armed, the Camisards rushed to

the stables, and mounting their horses bare-backed, rode off without saddles, bits, or spurs; thus they were soon after taken in a deep hollow way, and compelled to halt and dismount. Planting his back against an aged olive tree, Roland made a desperate resistance, to every summons of 'Rendez vous! bas les armes coquin!' replying by a blow of his sword, or shots from his pistols, a row of which he carried in his girdle. He slew several dragoons, ere one by a musket-shot brought him down, by a mortal wound, on which his comrades threw themselves above his body, and were seized and bound.

On the 16th of August his body was dragged at the tail of a cart into Nismes and burnt, while five of his companions were broken alive on the wheel around his funeral pyre. Many Camisards perished thus here, the most memorable executions being those of Catenat and Ravenel, who were burned alive, almost within sight of the battle-field on which they had defeated the Comte de Broglie.

Jean Cavalier found himself almost alone now, yet his spirit did not quail.

Marshal Villars had now come to the conclusion that the warfare seemed likely to become interminable; that it was possible to harass the hardy mountaineers of the Cevennes, but not to conquer them. So resolute was the spirit of the Camisards, so impregnable their hilly fortresses, that all hope of ending the war so long as one was left alive, was relinquished by this able officer ; and we are told that in the heart of Cavalier, who beheld the sufferings of the peasantry from incessant toil and famine, there rose a great longing for peace, if it were possible with safety and honour ; and on ascertaining that 10,000 of the Huguenots were ready to lay down their arms and submit to the king, he consented to hold an amicable parley with any officer the latter might send.

Cavalier's first interview was with Lalande, who was sent by Marshal Villars. ' Lalande surveyed the worn garments and pale cheeks of the young hero, whose deeds had reached the ears and troubled the mind of Louis XIV., in the midst of his mighty foreign wars ; he looked upon the bodyguard of the rebel chief, and saw there, too, signs of poverty and extreme physical suffering, and believed that he knew how to treat with men in such a condition.'

He proffered a large sum in gold, not a coin of which Cavalier would touch, though he allowed his followers to accept it for their starving wives and children ; and he made preliminary arrangements with Lalande for a final interview with the Marechal Duc de Villars.

It was in the summer of 1704 that the latter, the renowned antagonist of Marlborough, entered the garden of the Recollets, at St. Cesaire, near Nismes, the site of which is now occupied by a theatre, to discuss peace and war with 'the Boy-General,' Jean Cavalier, who, resolved to produce all the effect he could, appeared on this occasion magnificently mounted, with a richly-laced coat, and a hat plumed with white feathers. Cavalier's young face looked sad, we are told, and the tone of his voice was melancholy, 'and Villars looked on him with a deep admiration and sympathy.'

On this occasion Cavalier's bodyguard was a mounted force of Camisards in white tunics.

The result of this memorable conference was, that the insurgents laid down their arms on the assurances of justice and tolerance in religion to the persecuted Protestants of the Cevennes, and flattering promises of reward and rank in the army of France to Jean Cavalier ; but neither one nor the other was destined to be kept or fulfilled, and the Place de Boucarini, at Nismes, was soon deluged with the blood of all who fell into the hands of the Government. The Camisards now repudiated the treaty made by Cavalier, and, finding himself reviled by many of these on the one hand, and neglected by the Court on the other he became an exile, and entered the army of Queen Anne at the head of a regiment entirely formed of Huguenots.

As a colonel, in his twentieth year, he fought in the British Army in Spain at the Battle of Almanza, under the Earl of Peterborough, and there, in the defeat, his battalion of Camisards was almost cut to pieces by the victorious French, and there young Guillot, its major, died sword in hand.

Of the after life of Cavalier we can trace little. It is only known that by the British Government he was made Governor of the Isle of Jersey, and died at Chelsea in the May of 1740.

It has been more than once asserted that he died *in* the Hospital a pensioner, which is a mistake the records there distinctly prove.

In the year before his death, on the 2nd of July, he and his countryman, Colonel Balthazar Rivas de Foisac, were appointed Major-Generals in the British Army.

THE

BUGLE-BOY OF BADAJOZ.

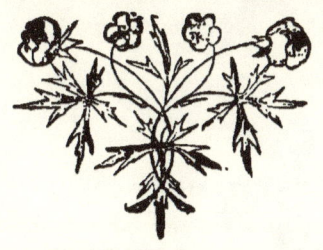

'MOTHER! mother! come out of the cold ground; come to your little José, who is so lonely now!' wailed a boy stretched on his mother's grave, while wetting with his tears the flowers that had been laid there, and the green turf, into which he dug his little hands in the wildness of his great grief.

It was in the cemetery of the Penha Convent at Cintra, and when ravaged Portugal lay wasted and bleeding under the feet of the French army, led by Marshal Junot, the Duc d'Abrantes, to Lisbon, in 1808, a period that seems long ago now, yet was fresh enough in the memory of our fathers.

It was on a glorious evening in autumn, and the hill of Cintra, the base of which is clothed with wood, but which terminates in loose crags and splintered pinnacles, was bathed in warm light, while every fissure was covered with amaryllis and aglow with crimson geranium, and giant evergreen oaks and cork-trees were intertwined with vines, all adding to the beauty of the scene.

On one hand towered up the hill with the Penha Convent, on the other were the ruins of a Moorish castle ; but the sunshine and the scenery were lost on the orphan boy. He saw only his mother's grave, and all the rest of the world seemed dark to him indeed.

'Look up, my boy,' said a voice, as a hand was kindly laid on his neck, and, rising from the turf, he found himself face to face with an officer of Cazadores, or Portuguese Light Infantry. He was a handsome and pleasant-looking man, clad in green uniform faced with scarlet, and wearing silver epaulettes. 'Who lies here that you weep for ?' he asked.

'My mother,' replied the boy, in a tone of infinite tenderness.

'And your father ?'

'Was De Castro, the guerilla chief, whom the French shot at the gate of the Torre Vilha. You have heard, perhaps ?'

'Yes ; he was taken prisoner in Lisbon ; a brave fellow—I knew him well,' replied the officer, with kindling eyes and lowering brow.

'My mother never held up her head afterwards— and—and three days ago she left me—and—and they brought her here,' said the boy, with a fresh fit of heavy weeping, as he pressed his knuckles into his inflamed eyes.

In tatters, and dusky in complexion, yet rich in colour, like the beggar-boys of Murillo's famous picture in the Dulwich Gallery, he was a handsome little fellow, with a clear olive skin, sparkling eyes of the deepest hazel, and thick, wavy black hair.

'Have you no brother or sister?' asked the officer, patting his uncovered head, for poor José was without hat or cap.

'None now. I had a sister once.'

'And she?'

'Was carried off by the French voltigeurs, and was never seen again. Poor Theresa!' said the boy, in a gasping voice.

'And have you no home, my little fellow?'

'None, but the church porch.'

'Then come with me, and I will find you another.'

'Where, senhor?'

'Under the colours of His Majesty Pedro the Third.'

The boy's face lighted up. It was too soon for him to despair yet; he had youth and hope, 'youth, with which the linen folds seem robes of purple, the chaplet of cowslips becomes a monarch's crown, and the wooden bench is as an ivory throne of empire.'

So little José Francisco de Castro, for such was his name, gave his hand in confidence to Captain Dom Pedro de Lobiera, and became a bugle-boy in the Seventh Regiment of Cazadores, among the Portuguese troops under the gallant Marshal Beresford, and destined to co-operate more immediately with that division of the British army which, led by Lieutenant-General Sir John Hope, took possession of Lisbon in 1808.

A curious combination of wrath and exultation made José's heart beat tumultuously on the day he first assumed his uniform, and he slung with a green cord over his shoulder the bugle with which he was to summon his comrades.

He had an admirable ear for music, and soon mastered all the many bugle-calls requisite for the manœuvres of light troops in the field, and by his coolness and bravery, while yet in his teens, became a prime favourite with his captain, with his colonel, the Viscount de Sa (whose 'orderly bugler' he became), and with the whole of the Seventh Cazadores he became a species of regimental pet.

When the battle of Salamanca was won by Wellington in the glorious summer of 1812, when we

attacked the Duc de Ragusa, and when Park's
Portuguese column was foiled in the first attempt to
storm the Arapiles, two steep, rugged, and solitary
hills that overlook the plain, it was José's bugle
sounding the 'rally' amid the hottest of the fire that
caused the southern hill to be re-won ; and when
Marshal Beresford was unhorsed and wounded in the
leg, while charging at the head of the 11th Light
Dragoons, and again while leading a Portuguese
brigade, it was 'José de Castro, a bugle-boy of the
Seventh Cazadores,' that helped him to remount, as
the *Portuguiz Telegrafo* of that week records.

On the plains of Talavera de la Reyna, at the
heights of Busaco, and by the green hill of Albuera,
when the Anglo-Portuguese army fought Soult—that
memorable hill, by whose slope, at the close of the
terrible day, the men of our old 'Die Hards' of the
57th were seen lying in two distinct ranks, dead but
victorious—the Seventh Cazadores, when wavering
under the dreadful fire of the French infantry, and
menaced by the heavy cavalry of Latour-Maubourg,
were rallied in square by the bugle of José de Castro.

He was ' ever foremost in the path of danger,' says
the *Jornal de Commercio* of Lisbon ; 'and the notes of
his bugle were heard in many of the desperate onsets
and bayonet charges of those well-fought fields.   In

all these actions he did his duty ; but his name ought ever to be remembered for a deed of valour, for which, at the time, he gained well-merited applause, and which was long afterwards passed from mouth to mouth whenever the terrible siege of Badajoz was mentioned.'

It is to the third siege of the city that the paper refers.

'Give me your hand, José,' said the Viscount de Sa on one occasion. 'What a boy you are! You beat the trumpeter who blew two trumpets at once at the siege of Argos.'

As yet he seemed to have a charmed life ; no ball had ever touched him. He was a good, devout, and very grave boy, for, as Captain de Lobiera said, he believed 'that the spirit of his dead mother accompanied him wherever he went.'

It was on the 6th of March, 1812, that the army of Wellington broke up from its cantonments, and, ten days after, crossed the Guadiana, and three divisions, under Beresford and Picton, at once invested Badajoz, then garrisoned by five thousand men under Generals Phillipon and Vaillant, whose tenacious resistance caused some uneasiness to the British leader, as a defeat under its walls might have seriously disarranged all his plans for the future.

Before the Seventh Cazadores entered the trenches they had halted a few miles from Badajoz, after a long and harassing day's march. The rain fell in torrents that night. Amid the misty gloom, in the distance, the guns of the beleaguered city were seen to flash redly out upon the night, and weird was the glare of the port fires as they sputtered on the gusty wind.

All that comfortless night, José, like the rest of his comrades, spent the weary hours in the open air. He placed his canteen on the ground, put his knapsack above it, and, thus improvising a seat, strove to sleep, with his greatcoat and blanket spread over his shoulders for warmth. And when the chill gray dawn came, he was so stiff that, at first, he could scarcely place the cold mouth of the bugle to his lips.

'Now, my men—la générale!' cried the Viscount de Sa, as he leaped on his horse, and the buglers, at the head of whom stood little José de Castro, poured clearly and melodiously on the morning wind, 'the générale, 'that old warning for the march—a warning long since disused in the British service, where it was well known once.

Then the Cazadores took the road for Badajoz, and that night were there in the trenches.

It is recorded of José that before the Cazadores

marched that morning he and a comrade bugler, Diaz
of Belem, gave up the little pay they possessed to
repair the loss of a poor woman whose hen-roost had
been pillaged of its inmates in the night.

The early weeks of 1812 were cold and rainy at
Badajoz, and the howling tempests of wind often concealed at night the noise of the shovels and pickaxes,
as the troops broke ground, within a hundred and
sixty yards of Fort Picurina, and pushed forward the
trenches, till they achieved an opening four thousand
feet long—a work of five days' duration, under a
dreadful shower of shot and shell.

Our artillery had succeeded in making a practicable
breach, by which the columns of assault might enter
whenever the order to advance was given ; but the
position of the enemy was strong by nature, and made
more so by art.   Enormous beams of timber, loaded
shell, huge stones, hand grenades, cold shot, all to be
launched from the hand, with relays of ready-loaded
muskets, were there, for those who were to keep the
breaches ; in these, too, were hundreds of live bombs
and sunken powder-barrels, ready to blow an assault-
ing force to pieces ; and it became evident that the
chances of that force proving successful were small,
unless some of the unforeseen accidents of war turned
the tide in their favour.

This point, say the Portuguese, it was the good fortune of José de Castro to achieve. For the actual truth of the episode which won him the name of 'The Bugle Boy of Badajoz,' we do not vouch. There is not a word of it in Napier, or in the despatches of the Duke of Wellington; but yet it was universally believed in the army of Marshal Beresford.

It is related in history that when the final, and, to so many, fatal, night of the 6th of April came—that awful night of horror and of triumph when Badajoz was won—when more than two thousand of our officers and men perished in the breaches alone, and when the heart of the 'Iron Duke' gave way to a passionate burst of grief for the slaughter of his gallant soldiers—on that night, we say, the 'unforeseen accident,' recorded by history, was a feint attack unexpectedly becoming a real one; but the Portuguese have it that José de Castro, being of an inquiring turn of mind, and having, during his service, had many opportunities of hearing the French bugle-calls, had learned them all to perfection, and now resolved to turn his knowledge thereof to good account.

After a lighted carcase, composed of the direst combustibles, and of giant size, had been flung blazing from the walls by the French, compelling the assault

to be anticipated by half-an-hour, when the stormers
neared the great breach, José and his comrade,
Diaz of Belem, advanced with the rest of the Cazadores.

When Diaz was in the act of taking some brandy
from his canteen, a sixteen-pound shot took off his
head. Yet, bugle in hand, José kept on, resolved to
put in practice the scheme he had formed, and with
which he had acquainted his colonel, the Viscount de
Sa, and his captain, De Lobiera.

As leaves are swept before a tempest, the stormers
came sweeping up the rough *débris* of the breach
covered with dead and wounded men, encumbered by
these at every step, shells bursting, shot and grenades
falling among them. Their shouts were terrible ; the
yells of the French more terrible still ! Up, up they
went, till they found the perilous gap was crossed by
a glittering, dreadful, and impassable *chevaux-de-frise*,
composed of sword-blades, keenly edged and sharply
pointed, fixed in ponderous beams, chained together,
and strongly wedged in the shot-riven ruins. Beyond
it were masses of the French pouring in their deadly
fire, sweeping the gap with sheets of lead as the wind
sweeps a tunnel.

Under the *chevaux-de-frise* the gallant José contrived to creep unseen, and, getting beyond it, to

conceal himself among a heap of dead. On again he crept, his dark blue uniform, splashed with blood and clay, enabling him to pass unnoticed among the French, till he reached an angle of the ramparts.

Then he put his bugle to his lips and blew loudly and clearly, again and again, above the awful din of the assault, the French *recall !*

On this the French gave way, fell back, and eventually fled across the river into Fort San Christoval, where, next day, they surrendered as prisoners of war to Lord Fitzroy Somerset, the future Lord Raglan of Crimean fame.

The action of José de Castro, say the Portuguese, was noised about, after the surrender of Badajoz, until it reached the ears of the Commander-in-Chief—the great Duke—who sent for him, and presented him with a sum equal to a hundred guineas English, which, in consequence of his youth, Captain Pedro de Lobiera was to pay him in small instalments. It is also said that the Duke gave the money from his own private purse. José also received a good service medal, and the Portuguese decoration No. 3.

He was now only eighteen, and the honours he received might have turned an older head ; but he continued to be as grave, modest, and well-dispositioned as, when a boy, Captain de Lobiera found him beside his mother's grave in the cemetery of the Penha Convent at Cintra; and while many were promoted to commissions, he followed the fortunes of the Peninsular army with his bugle slung at his back.

That bugle was heard on the plains of Vittoria, and among the passes of the Pyrenees, where De Castro was wounded and conveyed to the town of Elizondo. There, while stretched on a pallet of straw, in the vestibule of a convent, which had been turned into a military hospital, he was attended and nursed by a lay sister, who turned out to be his sister Theresa, who had been carried off by the French, but had achieved her escape after their defeat and total rout at Vittoria.

It would be difficult to describe the mingled joy and grief of such a meeting; but both were of brief duration. As soon as José was reported fit for duty, he rejoined the Seventh Cazadores, with whom he served at Nivelle, Orthes, and Bordeaux.

His bugle was heard for the last time in battle near the hill of Toulouse, when he sounded the charge by the order of the Viscount de Sa. In that advance the latter fell wounded from his horse, and, seeing that Captain de Lobiera, the next senior officer, was defenceless, his sword-blade having been broken off near the hilt by a ball, he gave him his own, saying :

'Lead on, De Lobiera! forward, the Cazadores! I can do no more to-day.'

And once again the bugle of José sounded the command to charge.

When the army was disbanded at the peace, José endeavoured to support himself by teaching music, but in a way so humble that he led a life of privation and penury, and sought, in vain, a pension from the Portuguese Government.

It was at the little town of Golega, on the Tagus, in Portuguese Estramadura, that we last heard of 'the Bugler of Badajoz.' This was more than twenty years ago, and he was earning a precarious livelihood by teaching the cornet.

He was then an old man, bent with years and infirmity, and had for the last time renewed his prayer for a pension to the Portuguese Government. 'Let us charitably hope it will be granted,' said a writer in the Lisbon *Jornal de Commercio* of that year, 'for there is now in the Ministry a soldier who has not forgotten the part he bore himself in the bloody episodes of the Peninsular War, one who has left an arm on a gory battlefield, and whose hearing has been destroyed by the thunder of artillery—the noble and valiant Viscount de Sa (the son of his old colonel). This gallant soldier will yet have ears for the petition of the poor *trombadero,* and be able to award him the meed he merits.'

THE

VOYAGE OF THE 'BON ACCORD.'

VOYAGE OF THE 'BON ACCORD.'

MY name is Bob Slingsby, and in the autumn of last year I was senior apprentice, or midshipman (for we wore a smart uniform), on board the good ship *Bon Accord* of Aberdeen, freighted from London to Hong Kong, and a few who may survive to read these lines will recall the story I am about to tell—the plain un-varnished one of a sailor boy (I was then only sixteen) in the Indian seas.

We had left Swatow on the 24th of September, after getting on board a pilot, who was the cause of all the mischief that followed.

The *Bon Accord* was a fine full-rigged clipper ship, of Aberdeen build, 900 tons, coppered to the bends, with masts that raked well aft ; she was straight as an arrow in her planksheer, and was well armed, for .there are some ugly customers to be met with in these seas beyond the ordinary track of our cruisers, as we found to our cost.

The ship's company consisted of Captain Archibald, a good and resolute seaman, who hailed from the port of Leith ; three mates, the doctor, Joe Ruddersford, boatswain, two apprentices (myself and my chum, little Charlie Newcome, for we were three short according to our tonnage), and thirty men—thirty-eight all told, and a few lubberly Lascars who all bolted when the first sign of danger came.

We had been well warned on nearing Hong Kong to keep a bright look-out for Macao piratical boats, and particularly for one large lorcha manned by only such desperadoes as are to be found about these shores ; and the captain of which, we were informed— Long Kiang by name—was as great a ruffian as ever figured of old, when Hong Kong was named by the Spaniards the Island of Ladrones, or thieves.

In a copy of the *China Mail* brought on board at Aden, we read a description of Long Kiang, which told us that he had been pierced and scarred by many wounds ; that one of his eyes had been scorched out by gunpowder, and that his left arm, having been severely shattered by a shot from a swivel gun, had never been properly set, the fragments had worked themselves out, and this gave him the singular appearance of having an arm and elbow adhering to the shoulder by the flesh and tendons alone ; yet this arm possessed double the strength of his right, and it was his boast that he had slain more men by it than with the other.

We made the name of Long Kiang a kind of joke— a bogie—on board during the voyage through the bay of Bengal and into the China seas, and had nearly forgotten all about him, when without other adventure than a foul wind or so we reached Swatow, some fifty miles distant from Hong Kong, and after anchoring for a little time, left it, as I have said, on the 24th of September, with a light fair wind, and by sunset had made an offing.

As evening deepened upon the crimson sea, the wind became lighter ; then it fell calm, and the fore and main courses were hauled up, while the top-sails were left to flap idly against the masts ; and now it was that a native boat came alongside with a pilot, who offered to take us to our destination for a certain sum in British money, and his services were accepted by Captain Archibald, to whom he showed, of course, good and well-attested certificates.

No trousers covered the long, lean, mahogany-coloured legs of this official ; an ample abba was rolled round his body, and a tattered keffiah, of no particular hue, thrown loosely round his head, partly muffled his face, so that we could see but little of his features.

The wind freshened after a time ; we let fall the courses and stretched them home, glad to make way on the ship; which had been drifting with a current.

Instead of standing by the binnacle and giving instructions to a steersman, the native pilot grasped the wheel unaided in his powerful hands, and from time to time it seemed to me that he cast his eyes oftener to the shore than aloft to keep the canvas full. As he stood there between us and the moonlight, his tall and muscular form and fantastic dress, when viewed in dark outline, had something weird and mysterious about them, and so thought Charlie Newcome, who was watching him narrowly, as we stood on the starboard side of the quarter-deck.

The mate of the watch was forward, looking after the 'ground tackle' and large anchor, and the captain was below, when suddenly Charlie, on whom the tall, stark figure of the stranger seemed to make an impression, twitched my sleeve and whispered :

'Look, Bob ! look now ! By Jove ! isn't he like— like——'

'Like who ?'

'Long Kiang, that we talked so much about—the fellow described in the *China Mail.*'

'You've got Long Kiang on the brain,' said I, laughing ; but the laughter ceased when I *did* look.

The light breeze had partly deranged the Arab-like keffiah that enveloped his head, and by the rays of the binnacle lamp we saw that he was minus the left eye, that the whole of that side of his face was distorted as if scorched by powder, and for a moment or two the strange malformation of his left arm was distinctly visible, as he gasped one of the under-spokes of the wheel.

'It cannot be,' said I. 'How about his certificates, Charlie ?'

'Another man's papers—stolen, no doubt.'

'If he should, after all, be Long Kiang,' I began, and then paused, for as I spoke the name seemed to catch his ear, and he turned on me his solitary eye, which in the moonlight glistened redly, like that of a rattlesnake. A knife of portentous length was in the same sheath with his chopsticks, a knife suggestive of cutting other things than yams or salt junk.

'Won't you youngsters turn in ?' said the mate, coming aft. 'You are both in the middle watch.'

'Thank you, sir ; not just yet,' said I, for, truth to tell, we were disposed to be wide awake as weasels.

Long Kiang had been such a standing joke during the latter part of our voyage—at least after leaving

Aden—that neither of us, whatever we thought, ventured to tell our fears or suspicions to the mate, or to the men forward. While we were talking to the mate, the captain, who had come on deck, called him to the port side of the ship, which was going before the wind, but very slowly.

The captain was a tall, stout, and well-built man, with a florid complexion and a mass of iron-grey hair, luxuriant as when in youth, and likely to be so for years to come. There was an air of sturdy Scotch power and strength of mind and body about him that showed at once his resolute will and energetic brain.

He and the mate of the watch were in close conference at the port quarter, and looking at some object with an interest that soon became anxiety after they had resorted to the use of a night-glass, on seeing which the tall pilot grinned and showed all his white teeth like a row of dominoes.

'It is a lorcha—full of men, and evidently dodging us—a Macao lorcha, too,' said the captain, in a low voice. 'You see that craft?' he said suddenly to the pilot, who had evidently for some time affected not to do so.

'Si—si—yaas—senhor,' he replied in the broken lingo peculiar to Macao.

'And what do you think of her?'

'That piecey boat makey fightey if you meddle with her,' he replied quietly, in what is called 'pigeon English' in these regions.

'Oh, she will, will she?' exclaimed the captain; 'bring the starboard tacks aft. Keep the ship away a few points.'

But the breeze was so light that the lorcha was able to pass and repass us with ease, on each tack coming nearer us, and, indeed, it became but too evident that the steersman handled the ship in such a way that in a short time the stranger would be quite able to overhaul us. She was already within half-a-mile of us when Captain Archibald roughly accused the pilot of treachery, and ordered the third mate to take the wheel. Ere he could do so the native uttered a shout, quitted the spokes, letting them revolve at will, throwing the ship in the wind, and then he leaped overboard.

An exclamation burst from all, for had the breeze been fresher the top-mast would have snapped off at the caps and left us a helpless wreck; but the captain —quick, ready, and powerful—caught the wheel in a moment, brought the ship again upon a wind, and without looking whether the traitor who had left us sank or swam, ordered the ship to be close hauled, as she was clipper-built, and to be steered 'full and by.'

Some of the watch said the lorcha had picked up our pilot. Charlie and I now spoke, and not a doubt remained in the minds of all that we had been deceived by Long Kiang, who, using the papers of some man he had robbed, and very probably destroyed, had steered the ship to a part of the coast of Swatow, where his vessel and men had been concealed in some bay or creek.

By nine p.m. the lorcha, which we knew must be manned by the ferocious half-breeds who are the sons of Chinese and Tartar slaves, with a mixture of Caffre and Portuguese, the refuse of Macao, was so close, that in the moonlight we could see them distinctly, and reckoned that she must have at least seventy of these on board, and all armed to the teeth!

Charlie and I had read much about pirates and wild adventures, and had longed to meet some; and now the time had come with a vengeance!

The Scottish firm to whom the *Bon Accord* belonged had wisely armed her well.

'Now, my lads,' cried Captain Archibald, as all the small arms were brought on deck, and the crew mustered aft the mizenmast, 'obey me; act well and steadily ; have faith in yourselves, for without it no man succeeds.'

A cheer responded, and under the care of the old boatswain, who had sailed with Archibald for more than twenty years, the guns were cast loose and loaded, and as some of our fellows belonged to the Royal Naval Reserve, they were at no loss how to go to work.

In common with several others, Charlie and I had revolvers ; but somehow, as I loaded mine, my heart was beating wildly, and, like Charlie Newcome, I thought of my mother, far away in Kent, as I had never thought of her before !

If captured, we knew that every soul on board would perish by a miserable death. Of a peaceful escape we had no chance, as the wind was so light, and many a glance was cast aloft to see how the sails drew.

The lorcha was stealing steadily after us in our wake now, for doubtless Long Kiang had told his crew of our guns, and knew that while she was kept astern they would be useless. Already the pirates were so close that we could hear their voices, and see knives, bayonets, and tulwars glittering among them, and towering amid the throng the tall and muscular figure of the ferocious Long Kiang, so we could have no doubt of the intentions of his followers now.

'She will soon be under our counter, sir,' said the old boatswain, 'and, as we have little or no steerage way on the ship, our eight-pounders will soon be useless.'

'Then let fly the starboard gun, and bring her to on the wind.'

Bang went the gun, its white smoke curling over the moonlighted water. A yell rose from the lorcha, and a red, flashing, and spluttering fire of musketry responded. No one was hit as yet, but white splinters were knocked off the woodwork on deck.

'Fill the yard heads! Stand off; Re-load, and then bring to again!' This manœuvre was repeated more than once.

Bang! bang! went the six-pounders from the port quarter. The yells were redoubled, and as every man who was not at the guns was busy with his breach-loading rifle, the work soon became hot indeed. While lying close to the gunwale, Charlie and I fired at random with our revolvers under the open leeboard; yet the whole situation was so strangely sudden—so un-expected and improbable—that it seemed as if all this peril was happening not to me—Bob Slingsby—but to someone else.

Close by us was the captain, busy with his Winchester repeating rifle.

The yells of the infuriated pirates, maddened by the slaughter we made among them, became every moment closer and more appalling, and united with the sound of the firing, made such a din that we could not hear ourselves speak.

In the foretopmast of the lorcha they were now getting their horrible stink-balls ready, while, by the use of sweeps, they came close under our stern, and we could see their fierce, dark visages, their glowing eyes, and white glistening teeth. These stink-balls are an odious composition of mealed powder, saltpetre, pitch, and sulphur, rasped hoofs burned in the fire, assafœtida, and all manner of foul-smelling herbs, and they threw them, smoking and flaming, on the quarter-deck by dozens, compelling us to retire forward, if we would escape suffocation.

Several of our men had now fallen, killed or wounded, and the crew of the lorcha came swarming up the mizen chains, over the quarter, and rushed on madly with swords, knives, and fixed bayonets; and then it was the Lascars vanished by running below, or leaping overboard.

In vain our stoutest seamen strove to stem the tide by bayonet and rifle, and the scene became to me agonising and terrific. The whole deck became slippery with blood.

Captain Archibald, bleeding from a wound, was shot again in the forerigging.

'Oh, my wife and bairns!' he cried, and fell dead on the deck. The chief mate fell next : another and another fell, and I found myself seeking shelter from the bullets near the forecastle bitts.

Who had fallen or who escaped I knew not, but the crew of the lorcha were now in full possession of the *Bon Accord*. Two or three dark faces appeared above the topgallant forecastle. Shots were fired at me, and with a prayer on my lips I fell into the sea, and then thought all was over with me. Mechanically I swam, and the miscreants kept firing at me and some Lascars who were in the water.

An oar belonging to the lorcha was floating near me. I grasped it, and got close to the forechains. All voices on deck, save those of the captors, had ceased. The firing was at an end. A few dead bodies, thrown overboard, plunged heavily into the water near me, and raised great phosphorescent circles and bubbles of water in the gorgeous moonlight. The breeze had freshened a little ; the reef points had ceased to patter upon the white sails which now curved gracefully out, and as the ship began to make a little way upon the water, I grasped the iron work under the forechains, and was carried with her.

Suddenly a rope's-end was lowered within my reach, and I heard a voice saying, in pigeon English :

' Comey up—me no killy you.'

I looked upward, and saw the terrible face of Long Kiang, with an indescribable gleam in his solitary eye, as it regarded me.   Aware that it was either for life or death, and that I might as well trust him as perish by a bullet or of drowning by exhaustion, I allowed myself to be drawn on board, and one of the first sights I saw was the body of poor little Charlie Newcome, lying near one of the maindeck guns.   Many dead and wounded pirates lay about.

On deck, I found myself the only living white !

Long Kiang grasped me by the arm with one hand, a long knife glittered in the other, and in a mixture of broken Portuguese and pigeon English, which would seem ridiculous to read, but was very terrible for me to hear, he questioned me about the ship ; where she was from, what was her cargo, and where any money was stored.   Finding that I was unable to give any account of the latter, Long Kiang, whose fierce eye when he was excited seemed to emit sparks as if struck from a flint—a peculiar pheno-menon—gave me a terrible blow with the hand of his boneless arm, and, falling senseless, I remembered no more.

Meanwhile the Macao men completely sacked the ship. Rice, biscuit-bags, beef-barrels, the fowls in the coops, wines, spirits, bedding, clothes, all loose ropes, and everything portable were carried on board the lorcha, and setting fire to the cabin, intending to destroy all trace of the ship by burning her to the water's edge, they finally shoved off to the lorcha, and getting the spirit casks aboard, began, like savages as they were—to make merry and have a night of it— and a night they *had* of it, that they little antici- pated !

About eleven p.m. I recovered, and found myself alone in the silent ship. The lorcha lay off about a quar- ter of a mile distant, floating on the calm and lonely moonlit sea, over which came the united noise of laugh- ter, singing, and shouts, as the orgies were continued in her bunks below and on deck. The odour of burning wood drew me to the cabin, which I found full of smoke; but on lifting the skylight, as well as the wound I had received would permit me, I found where the fire was smouldering, and after extinguishing it by a bucket or two of water, began to look about me with a heart torn by anxiety and apprehension. Lamps, chronometers, compasses, everything, were gone ; but had they remained, of what use would they have been to me?

On the blood-stained deck, where still some bodies, slashed and mutilated, were lying, their pallid visages looking doubly pale under the moon, I crawled forward, concealing myself under the bulwarks, to avoid being seen by the occupants of the lorcha, which was floating like a log upon the water.

In the forecastle bunks and elsewhere, to my intense joy, I found seven of our own men, all more or less wounded, coming forth now from their places of concealment—the old boatswain among them—but all doubtful what to do or how to act; for the slightest sound or movement in the ship might bring these wretches on board of her again; so we all cowered together in the forecastle, considering the future, and listening to the shouting and singing on board the lorcha. These seemed to grow fainter the nearer she was drawn towards the *Bon Accord* by the current; and some time after midnight they totally ceased, and the deepest silence reigned upon the sea, for the breeze had died completely away, and we heard only the slow flapping of the topsails, and the pattering of the reef-points above our heads.

Old Joe Rudderford, our boatswain, who was certain, he said, 'that every man Jack of them was drunk as a lord,' now resolved to take measures that would rid us of them effectually ere day dawned ; and, acting under his orders, we put them in practice thus :

The port-quarter boat was softly lowered, on the side that was *not* next the lorcha, and he, with two men and myself, with oars muffled, pulled swiftly, yet noiselessly, off to her. All our revolvers were loaded, and Joe, the boatswain, had with him the largest and sharpest augur he could find in the carpenter's tool-chest, and a fierce, triumphant expression shone on his grave, grim Scotch face, which had a chin and eyebrows that expressed resolution and firmness of purpose.

Never shall I forget the keen and aching anxiety and excitement of that time, as we crept towards the hateful lorcha, and at every stroke of our oars, at every respiration, expected to see some of her merciless crew start up and fire on us ; but all remained still—still as death—on board, as we got close under her starboard counter.

Our first mission was to cut away and scuttle her only boat, and while the boatswain, with strong hands and brawny arms wrenching round the cross-handle of the augur, bored a succession of large round holes between wind and water—with a few *below* the latter —two of our men with knives cut away all the star-

board shrouds or stays; and as we left her, and
pulled away to our own ship, the sea was pouring
into her, and we knew that unless the artificial
leaks were discovered and plugged she must surely
go down.

'Thank heaven, the breeze is freshening!' exclaimed Joe, as we regained our unfortunate ship, and
hoisted in the quarter boat; and, weak and faint as
we all were from wounds, soon Joe himself made sail
on her. During all the hours of that eventful morning we struggled to trim the ship, to coil up and clear
away the loose ropes and running rigging; to throw
overboard the dead men of the lorcha, which was now
settling down fast by the stern in the light of the
waning moon, and every moment her bow and bow-
sprit seemed to tilt up higher in the air.

At last, just as day began to break, a great commo-
tion seemed suddenly to take place on board. Cries
and shouts floated towards us on the freshening
breeze, and we could see Macaomen, Chinamen,
and Caffres rushing wildly to and fro, looking evidently for their vanished boat; and then their united
yells rent the sky, as the lorcha gave a great lurch to
port and anon went down with every man on board
of her. Many swam about for a time, but all sank
in succession, for the land was far distant, and we

were standing off north and by east before a pleasant breeze.

Next morning we fell in with a native fishing-boat with a crew of three men, who agreed, for the sum of five British sovereigns, to pilot us into Hong Kong, where we duly arrived, and came safely to anchor in the famous 'Red Harbour,' after a voyage that none of us are likely to forget.

We had some strange adventures on the way home, and with these I shall close my story.

Of our crew, after the encounter with Long Kiang, only seven, with the boatswain, Joe Rudderford, and myself, remained with the ship. We got a new captain, and made up our number again to thirty-eight hands, all told, from the company of a bark that had been cast away in the East Lamma Channel, and after they were shipped an interesting event occurred.

Among them was a miserable-looking young fellow who had been wrecked years before on the coast of China, and been kept as a kind of slave in a village near Tonquin. Joe Rudderford, observing the assiduity with which this young seaman—in gratitude for finding himself once more under the Union Jack —did his work, asked him what was his native place.

'Stonehaven,' said he ; 'I am a Scotsman.'

'Stonehaven! I am from there myself. What is your name?'

'William Rudderford.'

'Had you ever a brother?' asked the boatswain, with sudden agitation.

'Yes,' replied the other; 'but it is many a year since he last saw me, in our mother's cottage beside the Cowie water. Poor Joe! I wonder if he is alive now!'

'I am Joe—your brother Joe, Willie!' exclaimed the boatswain; and now for several minutes their feelings so overpowered them that they could neither of them speak till relief was given by tears; and each had to tell the other a long story, which lies apart from mine.

We left Hong Kong for New Zealand, with a mixed cargo, and dropped down the Lamma Channel into the China Sea, and after leaving the port for which we were destined, gladly trimmed our course for London, thinking by this time we had seen a good deal of the world of waters; but after leaving the harbour of Otago, and working to windward of a headland named the Nuggets, we stood away for the Southern Pacific.

From that time the people in Dunedin, which we

had left, and in London, for which we were bound, heard of us no more.

No homeward-bound craft reported having seen or spoken with the good ship *Bon Accord*, of Aberdeen ; no message concerning her came from the antipodes ; and, to torture the minds of our friends at home, the newspapers circulated all kinds of rumours—that bits of wreck had been seen, that we had among our cargo thirty tons of gunpowder, together with ' no end ' of petroleum and turpentine, commodities certainly calculated to produce the direst effects if ignited.

Month after month rolled on, and not even the most slender tidings came of the beautiful ship, and apprehension of a terrible fate deepened into certainty, in the loving hearts of all who had friends on board.

Meanwhile, where were we ?

In about the 50th degree of southern latitude we had for weeks pleasant gales and prosperous weather, so that we scarcely required to lift tack or sheet, but bore on merrily. Joe Rudderford and his newly-recovered brother Willie were inseparable, and the memory of little Charlie Newcome often came back to me sadly, especially in the night-watches, which he and I had so often shared together, for the ship and her surroundings were all the same in many respects as when he sailed in her. But we had not been long at sea before we discovered that our new captain was a bad seaman and a bully.

Every order was given with an oath. Myself and the other apprentices he called 'young whelps,' and even respectable old Joe Rudderford was often greeted with taunts which he received in silence, remembering 'the least said, the soonest mended.'

'He is a coward,' said Joe to me one day.

'What makes you think so?' I asked.

'Because he is a tyrant, and tyrants are always cowards. We'll never have a captain again so good as brave old Archibald.'

In that latitude a curious incident occurred to us. On a fine morning, when running on a splendid breeze, with our port tacks on board and royals and top-gallants set, Willie Rudderford, who had the watch, reported a sail on the weather-bow—a large ship, full-rigged, with most of her canvas set, but all in confusion, and some of it thrown slack. Her top-hamper suggested perfect disorder, and not a soul was to be seen on board, or responded to our hailing, after we edged close down to her.

We hove to, threw the mainyard in the wind, and Joe Rudderford, the first mate, and two hands, of whom I was one, boarded her in the dingy.

I shall never forget the nervous, anxious, exciting

and yet eerie emotions felt, as we clambered up the side of that silent ship.

She proved to be a new one of some 800 tons burden, laden with silk and indigo, to the value of £150,000, as her papers showed, bound from Calcutta to the Cape ; but how she came to be in these southern waters surpassed our comprehension. The oddest thing of all was that there seemed to have been a panic on board, for the deck and cabins were strewed with the clothes of ladies and children ; jewel-cases, jewels, and Indian shawls lay everywhere ; but the chief part of the baggage had been taken away. Still more extraordinary was it to find that she had been scuttled in every compartment, evidently for the purpose of sinking her. Private letters, that we had no time to examine, lay strewed about, and cloaks and coats, bonnets and caps, yet hung on the hooks in the cabin. But what was her story, or the fate of those who had abandoned her, or *why* they had done so, we were fated never to know ; for though our captain was in the highest glee at picking up so valuable a derelict, and proposed to put a few of the crew on board, and sail in company, a heavy gale came on after sunset, with thick clouds, and when day broke she was nowhere to be seen, and must have gone down in the night.

And now I come to the mystery of our disappearance.

Our voyage had been an exceedingly prosperous one till we reached the vicinity of the Crozet Islands, in the South Pacific.

This solitary group, 'placed far amid the melancholy main,' comprising the Marion Rocks and the Twelve Apostles, lies midway between Prince Edward's Island and the Island of Kerguelen, the abode only of seals and sea swallows, and twenty-two degrees west of the equally solitary St. Paul's, whereon H.M.S. *Megara* was cast away.

The Crozet Islands are all of volcanic origin—wild, rugged, and horrid in aspect, and nearly inaccessible. Their mountains rise in conical peaks to an elevation of from four to five thousand feet, and are covered by perpetual snow, while dense fogs frequently envelop their bases.

Before we came to this dangerous vicinity we had encountered a gale ; but it had spent its fury, and was subsiding. The prospect, however, of the winter evening sea (for though the month was July, it was the season of midwinter there) was cheerless—a darkening sky, and nothing living in view but a sea-bird or two, swimming and skimming over the white tops of the grey waves.

It had become evident to all on board that the
captain's work as navigator disagreed with that of
the mate and Joe Rudderford. He was 'out of his
reckoning,' but was wroth with anyone who dared to
hint that he was so ; and, to allay his chagrin, drank
large quantities of spirits.

With night dense fogs came down upon the sea ;
the captain walked the deck excitedly, keeping a glass
of spirits standing near him on the binnacle-head.
He often looked aloft, and talked to himself. At one
of these times, a little dog he had ran between his
legs and nearly capsized him. With a fierce oath he
took the poor animal up by the neck, and threw it
into the sea.

On this, the sailors looked darkly in each other's
faces, and felt sure that mischief was soon to
follow.

The mate and Joe Rudderford now suggested
respectfully, that, as the fog was deepening and the
wind freshening, some of the canvas should be taken
off the ship ; but, in a gust of fury, the captain, instead
of adopting their advice, had her trimmed before the
wind, the yards squared, and the fore and main
studding-sails hoisted to port and starboard. Willie
Rudderford was at the wheel.

The seamen grew pale, and muttered under their

breath as they obeyed the rash orders, and belayed the tackle.

'What do you think of all this, Joe?' I whispered.

Joe answered only by a grunt, whatever that might mean; but on board, it always seemed that a grunt from old Joe had more weight than a whole speech from any other man.

'I think we should take some of the canvas off her,' said he to me, after a pause, loud enough for the captain to hear.

On this, the skipper turned round furiously; but before he could say anything, there went up a cry through all the ship from stem to stern—I think I hear it still.

'May the Lord have mercy on us!' was the fervent prayer uttered by more than one brave fellow, as death seemed suddenly inevitable, when the ship went bump ashore with a frightful crash, and a horrible grinding sound followed.

'All is lost! Let every man shift for himself!' cried the helpless man who commanded us.

The three topmasts crashed off at the tops, with the fury of the shock, and with the yards and hamper fell heavily down over the yet inflated canvas, to port and starboard. Aloft we were a total wreck in a moment, and already going to pieces below.

Our new captain—a very different man from the gallant Archibald, who was killed in the fight off the coast of Swatow—was the first to perish, overwhelmed, apparently, amid the boiling surf in the dingy, in which he and the first mate tried to effect their escape.

Amid the gloom, I saw Joe and Willie Rudderford grasp each other's hard hands for a moment, as their minds, like mine, were doubtless filled with a thousand hurrying thoughts of home and distant friends— remembering, perhaps, former happiness, and contrasting it with the present danger and misery.

Horror had succeeded the first consternation and alarm into which the entire crew were thrown by this sudden and unexpected catastrophe. The afterpart of the hull was covered with water, but the bows were jammed hard and fast upon the rocks, where the boiling sea made clean breaches over them, washing away those who crouched there. By one of these seas I was swept overboard, and in a few moments I rose to the surface, feeling battered and bruised, with the salt water gurgling in my throat and whizzing in my ears.

I was washed towards some rocks, into the seaweed of which I dug my hands and clung to it, even with my teeth. For a moment the sea seemed to leave me, and I felt suspended above it. Then it rose again with tremendous force, and took me from my hold. I forgot all about the ship, and those who were perishing there ; I thought only of myself, of self-preservation, and the dread of death. In that supreme moment of terror and agony I seemed to live a lifetime !

Again I rose to the surface on the summit of the wave, which washed me along the slippery face of the rocks, and ere it descended I caught some seaweed again, above the point where I had been before, and again the water left me, suspended in air, and gasping for life.

Sea after sea rose again, but none reached me now, and the waves only hissed and burst against the rocks below me, as if infuriated at having lost their prey.

Once more I began to respire more freely, and hope grew in my heart—the hope that I might yet live.

Then the dread that I might be sucked down by some wave more powerful than the rest caused me to make an effort, which then seemed to me superhuman, to gain a footing ; and slowly and laboriously I climbed upward to where even the highest spray fell far short of me ; and in my heart I thanked God that I was safe, though where, or on what isle, I knew not.

In the mist and darkness I ascended some fifty feet to a species of dry plateau ere I ventured to stop and rest, and then I heard what, amid my own trouble and terror, had partly escaped my ear: the roar of the breakers below, with the shrill shrieks of our perishing crew.

'For pity's sake help me, whoever you are!' cried a voice a little below me; and, extending a hand to one of our people who had reached a shelf of rock, I assisted him upward, and he proved to be Willie Rudderford, sorely battered and bruised, having been dashed repeatedly against the cliffs; and now we began to ascend higher together.

I asked for Joe, the boatswain; but Willie only knew that they had been torn asunder by the waves that had swept him overboard, and he had not seen him again.

Panting and often breathless, drenched and sodden, clinging to the rocks, we continued to ascend, so far that even the booming of the sea began to sound faint; and then we lay down together, worn out, yet past all thoughts of sleep, to await the coming day and whatever might betide us.

The cold was beyond all description, and, but for the shelter an elevation of the rocks afforded us, we must have perished, as we lay there huddled close

together for mutual warmth, while ever and anon
Willie Rudderford lamented sorrowfully the too
probable loss of his brother.

Slowly the grey dawn stole in, and the mist that
enveloped the land melted away ; and, to make my
story brief, we found by degrees that seventeen of the
ship's company, including Joe Rudderford and our
two selves, had survived the catastrophe, and that we
were shipwrecked on the Crozets—those horrible isles
that lie in the Southern Pacific, out of the track of all
vessels !

We could scarcely congratulate ourselves upon our
escape, and some there were among us who bitterly
regretted that they had not perished with the rest.

Out of the fore-part of the wreck we contrived to
get some tins of preserved meat and a cask of gunpowder, after which she heeled over into deep water
and disappeared ; and a sigh escaped my lips as we
saw the last of our floating home—the good old *Bon
Accord.*

No island in the world could be more desolate than
the one on which we found ourselves. Lashed by
tempests, and surrounded by an ever-boiling sea,
never visited save by some adventurous whaler, that
solitary archipelago, the Crozets, does not possess one
human being !

Under Joe Rudderford, to whom we all turned now,
we began the dreary work of exploration, and found
that we were on a long, gaunt, and naked isle a few
miles in extent, without trees or verdure, and exposed
to surf and the bitter blasts of the Southern Arctic
winter.

Our boats had all been swamped or dashed to
pieces, so that we had no chance or means of crossing
to any of the larger islands which were visible, and on
this miserable reef we must remain and exist as best
we might.

Joe discovered a spring of pure water. 'Thus,'
said he, 'we are sure of the one great necessity of
life.'

Of food we had certainly one great source—the
sea-birds frequenting the spot. An incredible number
of albatrosses, frigate-birds, and gulls were resident
on the isle ; their eggs were found everywhere, and
they and their young, being all unused to man, became
an easy prey, as we could capture them by the hand
or knock them over by a stick.

'Thank Heaven,' said Joe, 'we have food and drink
provided, and it will go hard if our self-help and
sagacity as British sailors don't do the rest for us.'

Everything that was cast in from the wreck was
carefully brought on shore and stored up. By Joe's

orders, we placed a spare topmast on an eminence,
with a blanket, as a flag, attached thereto, and a regular
watch was told off beside it, to signal any passing
vessel. Rude shelters of stones were set up for weak
or ailing men among us; Joe divided us into messes,
and made arrangements for the distribution of the
birds, the eggs, and all else that was in our general
stock.

We required a moving and ruling spirit, and Joe
took that place.

By his orders we utilised the preserved meat-tins
as cooking vessels, and by partaking of certain coarse
herbs and wild grasses, boiled therein, we averted all
danger of scurvy.

For fuel we had at first the broken driftwood that
came from the wreck ; but this was soon, with all our
care, expended, and the cold would perhaps have
destroyed us, had not the indefatigable Joe discovered
that we could make fires of the bones and skins of the
seafowl ; and Joe, who was a well-read Scotsman, told
us all how Dr. Livingstone once fed the fires of his
steam-boat on the Rovuma River with elephants' ribs.

The success of our plan, to feed fires with the legs
of albatrosses, gulls, and kittiwakes, for the many
months that we did, proves the vast number we must
have caught ; but weary indeed were we of this daily

menu of eggs and oily sea-bird flesh, seasoned with salt obtained from the surf where it dried on the rocks.

I shall never forget the great horror that fell on us, when one of our little band died of a fatal gangrene, having injured his foot by a fall ; and as we buried him in the sea came the dread question, if we were all fated to perish in succession, who among us would be the *last* and lonely man upon that rocky isle ?

Save for the lucky accident that several among us had match-boxes in their pockets when quitting the wreck, we could never have lighted a fire! As the ship broke up, various things came ashore ; among others, a passenger's chest, wherein we found some blankets, knives, and spoons.

So passed away August and September, and all this dreary time, a keen look-out was kept from the first break of dawn to the last glimpse of sunset for any passing sail, as life depended upon rescue. We often marvelled whether any vessel ever passed in the night, as we had no fiery beacon to attract attention.

Finding themselves preyed upon, the sea-birds became wilder, and food grew scarce. It is easy to imagine the agony in which, with haggard eyes and wildly beating hearts, we twice saw the sails of passing ships; but they were 'hull down,' at a vast distance, and could not see our despairing signals.

At length there came a day—oh, never, never shall I or any who were with me then forget it!

The morning broke warm, fine, and sunny, and a shout came from the watch at the beacon, that 'a ship was close in shore!'

We started up from the shelter where we were sleeping. We could scarcely believe our eyes, as with prayerful hearts we stretched out our hands simultaneously and in silence towards her.

Yes—yes! there she was, little more than a mile distant, a gallant brig of considerable burden, with her courses, topsails, and top-gallant-sails set, close hauled on the port tack, on a gentle breeze.

We were incapable of shouting or cheering, so great was our emotion, and many of us burst into tears when we saw the sheets let fly and the fore-yard thrown in the wind, while, as an additional token that we were seen and that succour was coming, the Stars and Stripes of America were run up to the gaff-peak, and a boat was instantly lowered and manned.

She proved to be the *President*, whaler, who, fishing in that lonely sea, had by chance come near the isle, where her morning watch had at dawn seen the fragment of our tattered blanket waving in the wind.

14

We were speedily taken off, after having spent—as a tally kept by Joe Rudderford showed—exactly one hundred and fifty-nine days (a little more than five months) on an isle of the Crozets; and, with one accord, we all stood bareheaded, and thanked God for all His goodness to us, when we found ourselves safe on the deck of the American.

Her captain made us all welcome and comfortable; but as we were what he called 'a tight fit' on board, with his own ample crew, he landed us at the Cape of Good Hope. There I parted company with Joe Rudderford and his brother, who shipped on board a Scotch clipper to return to their own home, while I, with the rest of the survivors, came back by a passenger steamer to London, and found that my people had long since given me up as dead.

A TALE

OF THE

RETREAT FROM CABUL.

A TALE OF THE RETREAT FROM CABUL.

'IN the month of October—I won't mention the year, it seems so long ago—my then regiment, the gallant old 13th Light Infantry, with the rest of Her Majesty's troops who had the ill-luck to accompany us, were in the cantonments of Cabul.

'I can see them yet, in memory, on the plain in front of the mountain city, enclosed by walls and hedges, and bordered by those pretty villas which, in their perfect confidence in the people, among whom we had come to replace Shah Sujah on his throne, our officers had built for themselves and families ; on one hand the hills of the Siah Sung, on the other the haunted heights of Beymaroo, for it was affirmed that a demon of some kind did haunt them, and in the distance the city of Cabul, with its walls and streets of sun-dried bricks, the towering outline of its Bala-hissar, and in the background far away the summit of the Hindoo Kush, mantled with snows that never melt.

'When not on duty, or when I could not hope to meet Mabel—Mabel Berriedale, of whom more anon—I was fond of wandering about with my gun among the Siah Sung hills, and even into the Khyber Pass, in search of the *hill-chuckore* or Greek partridge, wild ducks, and quails, though frequently warned by Vassal Holland, a brother officer, who chummed with me in the same bungalow—and once, to my delight, by Mabel herself—that it was unsafe, because ugly rumours were afloat, rumours of which she heard more than we did, as her father was on the head-quarter staff—that it was both unsafe and unwise to do so, as a rising of the tribes against us was almost daily expected.

'What took us there? you may ask. Well, the same interest that may take us there again. With the view of frustrating the presumed designs of Russia, and securing as far as practicable the integrity of Afghanistan as a barrier against the aggressive attempts of that ever-grasping power, the Indian government resolved on the restoration of the Shah Sujah, a cruel and merciless old prince, who, after blinding with his own dagger his kinsman Futteh Khan, had been exiled. We replaced him on the throne with an army of 8,000 wild Beloochees to guard it, under the Shah Zadah Timour and Colonel Simpson of the Company's service ; but he soon excited again universal hatred and dislike among the fierce Afghan clans, who viewed us resentfully as unbelieving intruders. Thus the slender British force of 4,000 strong, which as allies occupied the cantonments I have mentioned, was in a perilous predicament—a very trap as it were, for between them and lower India lay savage passes, manned by hardy and warlike tribes, and everywhere the coming storm grew darker as the unwelcome Shah proceeded from one act of violence to another ; while his retention of a corps of Sikhs—the enemies by blood and religion of the Afghans—as a body-guard, roused all their rancour against him, and against us, whose commander was General Elphinstone, a feeble, ailing, and incapable old man.

'Such was the state of matters when Holland warned me of my rashness, and more than once declined to accompany me, and one day I certainly had an adventure—not an exciting one—but one which I never forgot, owing to subsequent events connected with it.

'Though October, the weather was fine and clear, for there, after February, there is only hoar-frost in the mornings usually, till the middle of March. Our band had been playing at the usual promenade in the cantonments, but I had quitted early; Mabel, whom I loved very dearly, but to whom I had, as yet, said nothing of that love, had, I thought, treated me coldly, so I took my gun in a pet, and went forth among the mountains, penetrating into one of the deep sheltered glens that open off the Khyber Pass.

'Either the birds were shy, or I was preoccupied; I saw only here and there a solitary crow and stork till I came to a little ravine, in which stood a Khyber tent of black blanket, with a large stone at each corner to prevent it being blown away. Its door, a mere mat of reeds, was open, and there came forth a pretty young Afghan woman—a wife, as I could see by her hair being braided and her trousers of some dark stuff; and though evidently but the spouse of some wild hill-man, she wore strings of Venetian sequins, and chains of gold and silver. She was fair and handsome too, though her nose was very aquiline, and her cheekbones rather prominent. As she proceeded to feed a Cabul pony, from a gathered heap of juicy herbage, I was just thinking what a pretty sketch the little tableau beneath me would make, when it received one or two rather startling accessions.

'Out of a grove of wild mulberry-trees, all unseen

by her, there came creeping slowly, stealthily, with cat-like action, and velvety paws, an enormous black wolf. I could, from the perch where I stood, distinctly see the hungry gleam of its eyes, its scarlet mouth half open, and the steam from its nostrils.

'At the same moment on the other side of the narrow ravine, there appeared a Khyberee, as his yellow turban and shaggy robe of camel's hair announced—a tall, strong and stately fellow, armed with his long juzail or native rifle, the lighted match of which was smoking. On his knee he took a steady aim at the wolf, but missed fire.

'A cry of rage and fury escaped him, but it mingled with the report of my unfailing double-barrelled Purdey, and struck by two balls just behind the ear, the wolf fell over on its back and pawed the air, in the agonies of death, while the Khyberee woman fled into her tent, and her husband, for such the stranger proved to be, came to me full of gratitude.

' "Sahib, from my soul I thank you," said he in Afghani, of which I had picked up a smattering. "You have saved my tent from a dreadful calamity, enter it ; from this moment you are the brother of Zemaun Khan."

'For though but a poor hill-man he deemed himself a Khan, and in evidence of his position in his clan, as being what a Scots Highlander would call a *dunniewassal*, he carried a falcon on his left wrist. He led me within his tent, where I was in turn gratefully thanked by his pretty young wife, for though the Afghans do not, like other Mohammedan races, universally shut up their women, they are as open to jealousy as other orientals, and at Cabul frequently resented the attention our fellows paid them—and this added to those errors for which the army of Elphinstone had to atone so terribly. A snowstorm came on, and thus I passed the night in the tent of Zemaun Khan, who would by no means let me depart.

'"You are welcome," said he, as his wife placed before us food and a jar of native wine, though neither would partake of it, "for in the fashion you have come, a stranger is a holy name"

'"And yet," said I, smiling, "we Feringhees fear you like us little."

'"Little indeed!" said he, as his brow grew dark. "Sahib, I have seen and known your people—seen them at their manly sports in the cantonments yonder; seen the wonderful boat that Sinclair Sahib launched upon the Lake of Istaliff, and the flying shoes he used thereon when ice covered the standing

water,' he continued, referring to a boat which was
built, and skates which were made by Willie Sinclair,
an ingenious " sub " of ours, to the great wonder of the
Afghans, who had never seen either before. " But
what brought you among our mountains? Indivi-
dually you English are fine fellows—noble fellows ;
but collectively we *hate* you," he added, while his eyes
and his set teeth seemed to glisten. " Could it be
otherwise with us, who see that you are unbelievers
who deem that Allah is but a name? But you are my
guest, let us not talk of these things. We shall have
our pipes of tobacco, and Nourmahal shall take her
saringa and sing us the ' Song of the Rose.' "

' She brought us cherry-stick pipes, obediently
assumed her native guitar, and sang to us, as her lord
and master suggested. The night passed pleasantly,
for the tent was in a sheltered spot ; and I got up
betimes to return to the cantonment, escorted part of
the way by Zemaun Khan, to whose wife I presented
one of the pretty charms that hung at my watch-
chain.

' As we parted within a mile or so of the cantonment gate, he again expressed his gratitude to me,
but said to me impressively, and with a low earnest
voice :

' " If you can quit this place for Candahar or Jellalabad go at once—go, and go quickly ; in three days, perhaps, it may be too late ! The hills will then be alive with men."

' "You say either too much or too little," I exclaimed rather angrily.

' " I have said what I have said. The web of your existence has been spun of the thread of sorrow, and the sword of the Afghan will rend it asunder."

' " If a rising of the natives is attempted," said I, " we shall not leave one stone of yonder Balahissar standing on another."

' "Be it so ; but," he added, pointing to the stupendous mountains, " you cannot destroy these— the fortresses given by God to the hill-tribes of Afghanistan ! And Ackbar Khan has sworn an oath that your whole host shall perish save *one man*, who will be only spared to tell the fate of his comrades !"

' I had already heard something of this before, and it had been a source of laughter, but for a time only, in our mess-bungalow in Cabul ; and that evening, when Vassal Holland and I were discussing my adventure, through the pleasant medium of brandy-pawnee and Chinsurah cheroots, he laughed loudly at the threat, like a heedless and handsome young fellow as he was, and stigmatised Zemaun Khan as " a melodramatic old donkey ! After traversing the

Bolan Pass under Willoughby Cotton, storming Ghuzni, and then taking Cabul, we won't be so jolly green as to take fright at the Afghans ;" adding, " and now to talk of something else. I may mention that your absence during the storm last night, and from parade this morning, caused much speculation in the lines, and, if it is any gratification to you, not a little in the villa of the Berriedales."

' " And he lay back in his long arm-chair, and watched alternately the rings of smoke from his cheroot as they ascended to the straw roof of the bungalow, and the expression of my face.

' " Was Mabel indeed interested ?" I asked, with heightened colour.

' " More than interested—agitated ! but I don't wish to fan the flame, for I fear it will be no joke to be the husband of such a girl as Mabel Berriedale."

' " Joke—I should think not, Holland."

' " What then ?"

' " A great joy ! But to what do your remarks point ?"

' " To begin with—her love of dress."

' " Pshaw ! every pretty girl has that—and she is lovely !"

' " In her opinion, her father the Colonel—or any father—is only the medium for supplying luxuries and pleasures, and to act as chaperon, if nothing more attractive can be had. A husband would soon come to be viewed in the same light."

'"Pleasures, luxuries!" I exclaimed; "there are deuced few of either to be had at Cabul. But you, the fortunate, happy, and accepted of her cousin Bella should not talk thus. You have surely been refused by her!"

'"Refused?" exclaimed Holland, laughing.

'"Yes," said I angrily.

'"I never asked her, even before I saw Bella; yet many an afternoon I have enjoyed her society very much."

'"I should think so; she would make a pleasant companion for a longer period than any Afghan afternoon. You mistake the girl entirely, in deeming her, as I know you do, vain, trivial, heartless, it may be."

Holland only continued to smoke in silence.

'"To-night at Lady Sale's, I shall put it to the issue, if I can," said I.

'"Both will be there."

'"Allow us then to don our war-paint."

'The claw-hammer coat, and waiter-like costume denominated "full dress," was not then etiquette in India; thus, we both set out in full uniform for Lady

Sale's reception, which, though given so far away from Western civilisation as the slopes of the Hindoo Kush, was pretty much like any other. The drawing-room of her villa was made up as like one at home as possible. The ladies of the garrison, and of the C.S., had all becoming toilettes, and native servants, in white turbans, were gliding about with silver salvers of coffee and wines. A buzz of conversation pervaded the room, and though the band of "ours," the 13th Light Infantry, discoursed "sweet music" in an anteroom, the tenour of the conversation, in certain knots that gathered around the manly and gentle-looking Sir Robert Sale, the commander-in-chief, General Elphinstone, and the luckless envoy Sir William Macnaghten, sad and thoughtful in aspect, was the reverse of lively, for

> ' " Great events were on the gale,
> And each hour told the varying tale."

Dost Mahommed Khan, late ruler of Cabul, was remaining a peaceful prisoner of the British Government; but Ackbar Khan, the most brave and reckless of his sons, had preferred a life of independence amid the wilds of Loodiana, and now he was said to be among the Khyber mountains, concerting means for the extermination of "the meddling

Feringhees," as he called the British, whom he had vowed to exterminate, all save ONE MAN!

'All this I had heard so often for some months past, that it somewhat palled upon my ear now, and I endeavoured to get near Mabel, who was seated on a sofa immediately under a chandelier, which shed down a flood of light upon her; and around her and her cousin were a crowd of gay fellows in all manner of uniforms, cavalry, artillery, and infantry; thus, I could barely touch her hand, and answer some questions concerning my adventure in the pass last night, questions which I saw she asked with dilated eyes, and considerable concern, when I had to give place to some one else, with whom she plunged at once into an animated conversation, as if to hide the momentary interest she had shown in me. This deeply piqued me, all the more as Vassal, in all the happy confidence of an accepted lover, was stooping over the pretty head and snowy shoulders of Bella, and eyeing me from time to time with a provoking smile. Mabel and I were on awkward terms. Her lover she knew me to be, though I had never declared myself, for two or three reasons, among the most weighty of which were monetary expectations from home; thus we had piques and little jealousies, even fits of coldness, that made our almost daily intercourse in the limited circle of the Cabul cantonments perilous work truly.

'Her face was indeed a sweet and winsome one, and once or twice, as a mass of her golden-brown hair, which her ayah had failed to adjust properly, fell suddenly about her neck, she gave a petulant shrug of her white shoulders, while her beautiful hands were upraised to confine the coils, showing thereby the taper form of her arms and the contour of her bust and waist, while many a "sub" looked fondly and admiringly on. Other handsome girls were present, and it was really something wonderful to see so much fair English beauty there in Afghanistan, at the very back of the world as it were!

'Her cousin Bella was a soft, yet sparkling little brunette, whose father had fallen at the storming of Ghuzni; since when she had lived under the wing and care of her aunt, Mrs. Berriedale.

'To simply eye her admiringly from a distance was not the *rôle* I had intended to adopt; but I resolved to wait my opportunity, when there might be some break in the circle around her, and was passing into the inner drawing-room, which was nearly empty, when I trod upon a pocket-book. It was a bijou affair—tiny, scarlet morocco, and gilt

—a lady's evidently. To whom could it belong? I looked round for Lady Sale, but she had left the room. The owner's name would doubtless be inside; ere I could think of opening it, the book opened of itself, where a leaf was turned down, and where I saw—*my own name*, written more than once, with another added thereto: "Mabel Clinton—Mrs. Robert Clinton."

'I trembled with astonishment and joy. She had been wondering how the name would look *written*, and written it was, in her hand, with which notes of invitation had made me perfectly familiar. I heard the hum of voices in the next room, the sounds of laughter, and the crash of the band in the ante-chamber beyond, as one in a dream, for the discovery now made was rather a bewildering one.

'That I had a place in her heart, that she was more than interested in me, and that she linked the idea of me with herself, I would not doubt, despite her occasional coldness and coquetries with others; but how was I to use the knowledge so suddenly, so unexpectedly won? It was alike dangerous to keep or to return the book, though surely she would never dream that I had opened and read it, but the hand of Fate had done the former for me; and if thrown aside, it would be found by others, and become a source of secret joking in the cantonments, so I placed it in the breast of my uniform, and seeing her left almost alone for a moment, hastened to capture her, and offer her my arm, which she accepted at once, and we proceeded slowly to promenade the rooms.

' "You have not been near me to-night," said she, fanning herself, though the air was cool enough.

' " It is so difficult to get near you ; you are always the centre of a circle in whose unmeaning gaiety I have not the heart to join."

' "You scarcely compliment me in saying this," said she, colouring a little ; " I was fond of gaiety, fun, what you will, when in Central India, and down at Calcutta, but here we have been *triste* enough. Cabul is simply horrible !"

' "And I wish, for your sake, and the sake of many others, that we were well out of it; but it was not of this everyday topic I desired to speak with you."

' "Of what, then ?" she asked in a low voice, though we had now reached the lower end of the outer drawing-room, where the windows were open to the floor, and gave access to a veranda filled with flowers, and the green jalousies enclosing which rendered it a species of corridor.

'My heart beat lightly, and I was on the point of saying something, I know not what—pretty pointed, however, when, in an evil moment, I drew forth her pocket-book, and said :

'"Does not this belong to you, Miss Berriedale? your initials are gilded on the cover."

'"It *is* mine!" she exclaimed, while blushing deeply, and then growing deadly pale, as she remembered what she feared I might have seen, and more, perhaps, that I had not seen ; "where did you find it ?" she added with some sharpness of tone.

'"Lying on the floor, yonder, in the other drawing-room."

'"And how long have you had it ?" she continued, with an increased hardness of tone which chilled me.

'"But a few minutes ; young ladies should be careful——"

'"Of what ?" she inquired haughtily.

'"Miss Berriedale," said I, in agitated voice, and endeavouring to take her hand ; but she eluded me, and even withdrew her arm, saying, "I must rejoin mamma."

'She rejoined the large group near the chandelier, with her whole manner and bearing totally changed, while I followed her completely crestfallen, with the eyes of Vassal Holland upon me, as if inquiring

whether I *had* put my fate to the issue, and what
had come of it.

'A vague sense of having incurred her displeasure
at the very moment when I was about to declare my
passionate love for her, oppressed me ; yet, when the
time for departure came, and the carriages and palkees
were announced, I hastened to cloak her, but she submitted in grim silence.

'"Will you pardon me 'if I have offended you?"
I whispered.

'"I have nothing to pardon."

'"Forgive me, then?"

'"I have nothing to forgive."

'"Good-night."

'"Good-night, Mr. Clinton."

'She did not even take my hand, and we parted.

'"What's up, old fellow?" asked Vassal Holland,
as we strolled away to our bungalow in the lines.

'"By Jove, I can't tell you."

'"You've not made your innings, any way?"

'"No," said I sadly and savagely ; yet I could
have enlightened him as to the situation, had I
chosen, but unless I could have ensured his silence
with regard to Bella, to do so might have made
matters worse.

'She loved me, I could not doubt it. But she

feared I had *read* the secrets of her pocket-book—
the dear, stupid words she had written half in play;
and all her maidenly modesty was up in arms, lest I
should take advantage of what I had learned,—
that she had given her heart to a man ere he asked
for it, and that if I wooed her now, it might only be
out of compassion or pity, melting into love.

'I could not doubt that, but for the unlucky advent
of the pocket-book, she would have permitted me to
love her, and have fully accepted me, with her uncle's
consent; and now—now for days she avoided me, and
began, that was patent to all in the cantonment, a
very deliberate flirtation with my friend Jack Villars,
of the Horse Artillery, a handsome but heedless fellow,
whom she had never distinguished before; and, though
I knew not quite why, the life of us *both* was embittered.
I was indignant that she should think so meanly of
me as to believe me capable of deliberately opening
her pocket-book and prying into her secrets, while she
was exasperated at her own folly in writing what she had
written. Had I seen it? doubtless she asked of herself,
and might have remembered that I had spoken of her
"initials;" and perhaps, had I made the most solemn
assertion that the wretched little book had opened of
itself, she might have failed to believe me.

'At last the route came for our regiment, with the

rest of Sale's brigade, to begin the march towards the province of Jellalabad ; and I shall never forget the morning of our departure. We were armed with old and unserviceable muskets, because our final destination was Britain, and General Elphinstone, a useless, obstinate, and incapable old man, said there was no use in taking new arms home. Our men were to march with their knapsacks, a new feature in Indian warfare ; and the officers reduced their baggage to a minimum, for rumour said the passes were beset, and the odds were heavy that not a man of us might live to reach the lower end of them.

'On the cold, dull, cloudy morning of the 10th of October our drums beat, and all in the cantonments at Cabul turned out to see us depart. Among other spectators on horseback were Bella and Mabel Berriedale, with the now inevitable Villars in attendance upon the latter ; and if aught could add to the sorrow, bitterness, and chagrin of a parting that would be final—as she was to be left behind in Cabul—it was to behold this !

'After forming my company I drew near her, and made some commonplace remark, to which she replied in the same tone. I failed to catch the expression of her face, as a thick Shetland veil was tied over it. How little could I think that it was conceal-

ing tears! Suddenly Sale's bugler sounded; the adju-
tant was about to tell off the battalion. I pressed her
hand; she returned the pressure firmly, and her voice
as she said "Good-bye" was utterly broken, and
seemed to be full of tears. I never, never forgot *that*;
but this was no time for explanation. I rushed to join
my company, and all that followed passed like a
dream. The brigade was wheeled into line—it broke
into sections—the bands struck up, and the homeward
march for England, as all our fellows fondly hoped,
began; and ere long, as we penetrated into the dark
recesses of the mountains, we saw the last of Cabul
and all our companions.

'I had but one thought—that Mabel Berriedale was
there, and that I should never see her again!

'Even the armed clans of Afghans that were seen
hovering so manacingly on the rocks that overhung
the passes could not draw my thoughts from Mabel,
the pressure of her beloved hand, and her tearful voice,
when it was too late—all too late!

'The following night some wounded fugitives
brought dreadful tidings to Cabul. Sale's brigade,
they asserted, had been attacked in the passes and
literally cut to pieces; how Sale himself and Colonel
Dennie had been wounded, and Lieutenant Clinton
of the 13th had been cut off, with a whole line of

skirmishers, by the Khyberees under Zemaun Khan.

'My poor Mabel fell fainting on Bella's breast when she heard of all this, and she now for the first time knew, what I knew not, and never might know, how really dear I was to her. The startling tidings brought to Cabul were not without some grains of truth.

'Hardy and trained, the 13th, or Prince Albert's Own, marched speedily and splendidly, setting an example to the rest of the brigade, and their chorusing merrily woke the echoes of the impending rocks; but no actual hostility was displayed by the warlike denizens of these until the troops were fairly entangled in the deepest, steepest, and most perilous parts of the passes.

'*Then* the cliffs above us seemed to become suddenly alive with men, chiefly yellow-turbaned Khyberees, who opened a storm of fire upon us that told with dreadful effect, strewing the whole tortuous path from front to rear with killed and wounded. So skilful too were these Afghans in the art of skirmishing, that save for the red flash of their matchlocks streaking the gloom, it was impossible to detect where the marksmen lay. Rocks and simple stones—some not larger than a 13-inch shell, sufficed to shelter the lurking juzailchee, who squatted down, showing, if anything, only the long barrel of his deadly weapon, and the tip of his turban. Then might be seen the hardihood, and the majesty, with which a British soldier fights!

'Cheerily rang out the bugles of the 13th, for "the leading companies to extend," and away the skirmishers swept over the precipices, scouring the terrible hills on the right and left, using the bayonet wherever an opportunity served ; and driving back the wild mountaineers, till, just as night was closing in, we came in sight of a mighty barricade of earth, stones and turf, built right across the narrow pass, for the purpose of cutting off all further passage or progress.

'Sale, who was suffering acutely from a ball in his leg, gave the order to storm it, and just as, with a loud cheer, the leading companies assailed it with a headlong rush, a ball struck me in the left ankle, and my shako flew off ; an invocation to heaven escaped me, I fell heavily, my head came in contact with the rocks, and insensibility rendered me oblivious alike of peril and agony, as our men swept over me to storm the barrier, which they did brilliantly, fairly opening up a passage to Boothak, and carrying off all their wounded save me. I had fallen unseen, and in the dark was left behind, while the flashing and reports of the musketry died out in the distance.

'Bitter and terrible were my first emotions, when the falling dew roused me in that savage place; bleeding, helpless, unable to stand or crawl, a prey it might soon be to Afghan knives, or the teeth of those wild animals which would soon scent the dead that lay around me. I was not left long to reflect. I had just bandaged my wounded limb with my handkerchief, when a party of Afghans passed. One uttered a hoarse cry, and was about to decapitate me by one slash, when another interposed, and I found myself the prisoner of Zemaun Khan.

'"Death to the Feringhee!" cried the astonished Afghans.

'"Hold, I command you!" said Zemaun; "he is my brother."

'"Is he not one of those who would send our chiefs in chains to the Queen of the Feringhees in London?"

'"He is my brother!"

'By his order I was conveyed, not unkindly, to a solitary round tower among the mountains, where I remained a prisoner for longer than I care to remember, with the terrible consciousness that I might be murdered at any moment of caprice, or kept a life-long captive, forgotten by all, while Mabel Berriedale became the wife of Jack Villars, or some one else.

'My adventures after this were so numerous that they would crowd a three volume novel.

'The ball in my ankle I contrived to snip out myself, nearly fainting as I did so. I then bound up the wound, which grew well rapidly; while that in my head was bathed and bandaged tenderly by the deft little hand of the wife of Zemaun Khan, who was full of pity for me, with much of gratitude for the service I had done her, and thus I had perhaps more of her society than the Khan might have relished; but he had much wild work to do among the mountains, and it was from her that I heard of what was doing at Cabul.

'"Sahib, your people will never escape; it will all be as Ackbar has sworn," said she in her soft Afghani, as she drew near me and spoke in a low cooing voice, lest others might overhear, in these rooms that had only hangings and no doors. "Sixty thousand citizens in Cabul, and all the mountain tribes around it are ripe for insurrection, and wait but the voice of Ackbar."

'"But our soldiers are brave, and our envoy is wise."

'"Was, you mean, Sahib."

'" How—is he dead ?"

'" Yes," replied Nourmahal, shaking her head, while all the sequins flashed and glittered among the coils of her splendid dark hair ; 'he was lured into a conference with Ackbar, my husband Zemaun and other Khans, by whom he was dragged away and beheaded, in the face of your whole troops, who are now hemmed up in their lines, a prey to hunger and despair, while the passes are full of snow, and all the country up in arms."

' I scarcely believed all this at the time, but she never told me aught save the strictest truth.

' Hunger, cold and peril ! Poor Mabel ! thought I. On how little will a lover dwell with delight ! The pressure of her gloved hand at parting, her broken tearful voice, which said more than a thousand words, and the remembered signature, all seemed to make her mine, and yet I never might see her more. I must have been reported among the killed, and as such wept for by poor Mabel, and in time to come would be mourned by my dear old mother in England far away.

' Every item of intelligence that reached that lonely tower was communicated to me by Nourmahal, but, I began to perceive, only when the grim Zemaun, with his baggy breeches, black fur cap, and shawl with its armoury of daggers and pistols, was absent. I began to perceive, too, that she was enhancing her great natural grace and beauty by a costume such as she had not worn in the tent, with a white silk camise and pink silk trousers, and a thin veil of muslin embroidered with gold, the use of which she managed with great coquetry, especially when she idled over the strings of her saringa ; and she made wonderful *œillades* under her long dark eyelashes, when singing the "Song of the Rose," and other ballads in her softest Afghani.

'"Sahib," said she one day, coming to me with her dark eyes quite dilated, "pardon and departure in peace has been offered to your people, if they will leave all their women in the hands of the Afghan chiefs; but they have refused, and only one cry is heard in their camp."

'"And that cry is ?"

'"'Let us fight our way down, sword in hand ! A few of us at least shall reach Jellalabad.' But they will never reach it," she added sadly ; "Aziz Khan and Zemaun Khan have beset their homeward path with 10,000 wild Kohistanees, and the Ghilzies—the fiercest of Afghan warriors—hold the heights that overlook it."

'I started to my feet as I heard all this, as if I

would be gone; but I threw myself back on the camel's hair divan in a species of despair, as I knew that the tower was guarded by men with loaded juzailchees that would kill at 800 yards. She regarded me wistfully, and drawing near nestled like a child by my side.

'"Has the Sahib a wife in yonder camp, that he looks so sad?" she asked shyly.

'"No."

'"A sister, perhaps?"

'"I have none."

'"That is well; you will have none to weep for."

'"How?"

'"Because, whether given as hostages in peace, or taken as spoil in war, the Feringhee women will become the gholaums—the slaves of the Afghan chiefs."

'My blood ran cold and hot alternately as she spoke, and something like an imprecation escaped me. She laid a hand upon my arm, and drawing nearer, said in her most winning voice: "But what is all this to you? If you have no wife, no sister, then what can the fate or fortune of the rest matter?"

'The name of Mabel rose to my lips, but died there, for a new light broke upon me with a knowledge of what my preoccupation of mind, during all

October and the subsequent weeks, had prevented me seeing; that, influenced by pity, gratitude, and the singular respect with which I, as a gentleman, treated her—a respect to which she was all unaccustomed—the wife of Zemaun Khan actually loved me; and the knowledge of this filled me with only confusion and dismay, for if he discovered the fact our lives were forfeited, and already some of his household might be suspiciously cognisant of it.

'"What is all this to you, I repeat?" she asked, her clasp on my arm tightening.

'"More than I can tell you," said I, covering my face with my hands, and striving to think.

'"Be comforted; in losing your friends, you have not lost all who may love you—you have still *me!*" she added in a low voice, as she laid her head in a nestling way on my shoulder.

'This was coming to the point with a vengeance, and adding incalculably to the perils that surrounded me; and how was I to temporise with this hotblooded and impulsive little oriental, whose sudden love might quite as rapidly change to bitter hate?

'"My God—could I but escape!" I exclaimed.

'"You can; but on one condition."

'"Oh, name it!"

' " Take Nourmahal with you !" said she imploringly ; " she would die if left behind."

' " And die she shall !" said the low, concentrated and terrible voice of Zemaun Khan, with a grim and terrible expression of face, suddenly appearing in the curtained doorway.

' A low wail escaped Nourmahal, who sank at his feet.

' " I have heard all !" said he sternly.

' " All ?" I repeated mechanically, and thinking the word might be my last.

' " Yes, all, Sahib, and blame not you."

' " Whom, then ?" I asked.

' " Her !" he replied laconically.

' " She has done no wrong !" I urged ; " I call Heaven to witness !"

' " Silence, Sahib ! No actual wrong, but she is morally guilty," he exclaimed, in a hoarse, fierce, broken voice, as he spurned her with his heavy Afghan boot ; and then, as she crept grovelling towards him imploring pity, but silently, like a dumb animal, he added, "and thus do I, her husband, punish her !"

' Then, quick as lightning, he drew, from among the bundle of weapons in his shawl-girdle, a dagger, and plunging it in her bosom, killed her on the spot.

16

A crimson torrent flowed over her white camise, while the horrible dagger remained in the wound. I say horrible, for the weapon was constructed in such a manner, that after being thrust into the body the blade, on touching a spring, separated into *three*, thus rendering extraction impossible.

'This tragedy appalled me, and I looked wildly round for a weapon, resolved to sell my life as dearly as possible. Zemaun Khan saw the action, and smiled bitterly.

'"Your life is forfeited," said he; "but not while under my roof. I swore to be your brother for saving the life I have just taken, though I might have obeyed the fourth chapter of the Koran, and immured her till death came; but such a process would be too slow for me," he added, grinding his teeth. "You have eaten of my bread and salt, and to that salt I shall be true till we meet among the mountains; and then woe unto thee, Feringhee! Your people are departing—go forth and join them; but their fate and yours is sealed. Go—I have said."

' All that passed afterwards seemed like a dream to me then. I gladly quitted that chamber of horror, where the poor girl-wife lay weltering in her blood; a horse was given me, and a heavy tulwar or native sword. A wave of the hand towards the hills was all the farewell accorded me by Zemaun Khan, and turning my back upon the solitary tower, I rode in the direction he indicated, which proved to be the Khoord Cabul Pass.

'Night was closing in among these stupendous mountains, which were then all covered with snow; but as I rode on partly at random, thinking chiefly that I might be pursued and destroyed by Zemaun Khan and some of his followers, the sound of firing in front began to reach my ear. It became quickly louder and louder as I proceeded, and ere long there opened before me the long dark vista of a snow-covered gorge, on both sides and in the centre of which thousands of muskets were flashing redly out amid the gloom, while their reverberated reports mingled with a most horrible medley of sound. The British troops were being attacked; I could not doubt it, and I rode on madly and furiously to join my comrades.

'This was the night of the 8th of January, and, as I afterwards learned, it was but two days before that our whole garrison in Cabul had begun one of the most disastrous retreats ever recorded in the annals of war!

'It had been finally arranged by Colonel Berriedale and the rest of the staff that, on the payment of

1,400,000 rupees to Ackbar Khan, Zemaun Khan, and the chiefs of the Kuzzilbashes and Ghilzies, that our troops were to march unmolested ; yet the first-named ruffian again recorded his terrible vow, " that every Briton should be exterminated save ONE, who was to have his hands and feet cut off, and be placed thus at the mouth of the Khyber Pass, with a written notice to deter all Feringhees from entering Cabul again."

'The helpless sick were left behind ; the ladies and soldiers' wives were all in dhooleys or on horseback ; and the number of souls who quitted the camp is estimated at 16,500 in all.

'As the troops marched on they were hemmed in and impeded by the hordes of Afghan horse and juzailchees, who with yells and shouts dashed reck-lessly through the ranks, in fierce and savage mockery at the wailing of the Hindustani camp followers, who saw their wives and children slaughtered before their eyes, or borne off, the prey of mounted warriors. H.M.'s 44th, with horse and artillery, under Brigadier Anquetil, formed the advanced guard ; the 54th, with some other horse and four guns, covered the rear, on which a fire of musketry was opened from the cap-tured cantonments. Soon the attack was general on every hand, and the retreat became a disorganised flight. Horse, foot, and artillery—men, women, children, baggage-horses, and ponies, were all wedged together in the narrow way, where the corpse-strewn snow soon became a bloody puddle, while a storm of matchlock-balls poured down on the helpless column as night closed in, and none could say who had escaped and who perished.

'The aged and dying Elphinstone, with the ruin of his army, halted amid the falling snow, without tents and food, by the margin of the Loghur stream, hoping on the morrow to clear the Khoord Cabul Pass; but it was already in possession of Ackbar and Zemaun Khan! With dawn the flight, for such it was, began again. Among the wounded was Lady Sale, who had a ball in her arm; and as Mabel had her horse shot under her, Colonel Berriedale mounted her on his own, and fought on foot, till a ball, unknown to his daughter, laid him low. A flag of truce was sent to Ackbar, who shot the bearer of it, the gallant Captain Skinner.

'Pretending he had no longer any control over the people unless hostages were given, Ackbar thus artfully got into his power, as such, General Elphinstone, the *whole* of the women of the army and their families, including Ladies Sale and Macnaghten, who were conveyed back to Cabul; while the army, thus degraded, continued its flight through the deep snow in the dark and shadowy gorges, into which the Khyberees and Ghilzies poured an incessant fire of rifles, till the Tarechee Jungle, or Dark Pass, was reached, where the whole 54th perished to a man.

'There it was I contrived to join our 44th, or what remained of it, for in one group 200 of it had fallen ; and then I learned those dreadful tidings, which made every heart in Britain throb, that the women of the army, among them my Mabel and her cousin, had been surrendered to the Afghans !

'"In all the world's history," said Jack Villars, "there will be no retreat recorded like this! That from Moscow had its survivors ; this from Cabul will have *none !* But have a cheroot, old fellow ; it is all I have saved out of my baggage."

'The terrible march was continued, and on every side the rocks re-echoed the cries of "Death to the Feringhees ! Death to the infidel dogs !" while the wounded were always stripped and horribly mutilated. After a brief halt, at which some ponies were shot, flayed, and eaten raw, on we struggled again, on and on, under a shower of shot that decimated us at every step, until we reached a place called Jugdulluck, by which time every officer of rank had perished ; and there, on a knoll, under Jack Villars,

myself, and another, the wretched survivors, men of
all arms, made a last despairing stand against the
enemy.

'"Keep by me, Clinton!" cried Villars, brandishing his sword; "we can die but once!" He had
barely spoken ere he fell forward on his face, choking
and dying, with a ball in his chest.

'Cheering wildly, we stood shoulder to shoulder,
as if to welcome death; many of us faint and bloody
with open wounds; but showers of matchlock-balls
rained on us, and the roll of death increased as the
men fell across each other in heaps.

'The sudden fury with which we resisted here
checked even the ardour of the hordes that assailed
us, and we were permitted to struggle down the
pass, leaving the dead or the dying at every step, till
the 13th of January, when *twenty* officers and
sixty privates, the sole survivors of Elphinstone's
army, unable to proceed further, made a halt on a
knoll at Gundamuck, near a grove of cypress-
trees.

'To all this violation of the laws of war, this terrible
treachery and lust of blood, was added a sense of
deadly horror as to *what* would be the fate of our
gently nurtured European women at the mercy of
men so savage. Imagination ran riot, the heart grew

still, and we could but hope that ere this, death had
put an end to the sufferings of all.

'"My poor Mabel!" I could but gasp, rather than
sigh, at the thought of her.

'Our ammunition was gone, we were too weak to
resist with the bayonet, and, led by Zemaun Khan,
the enemy burst in among us—a sanguinary mob—
and with the knife alone slew every man there but
myself and two other officers, who, being mounted,
broke through, sword in hand, though all more or
less wounded, and escaped by the speed of our horses ;
yet close at our heels came a score of mounted Afghans,
Zemaun among the number.

' They fired repeatedly at us, but their matchlocks
were useless on horseback, till some dismounted and
fired, taking deliberate aim over their saddles ; thus
my two companions fell, and were instantly decapi-
tated ; while I rode wildly, blindly on, with the blood
pouring from three wounds, and fast and fiercely
behind me came the pursuers, one outriding all the
rest—Zemaun Khan.

' Already the last of the pass had been left behind,
already the country was becoming more flat and
open, as I entered upon the plain, or rather valley,
where before me lay my only haven, Jellalabad, with
its minarets, domes, and those walls and bastions of

brick which had for months been held by the soldiers of Sale's brigade.

'Could I but rid myself of Zemaun, I might reach it. I checked my horse, and taking a Parthian aim at my chief pursuer with the last shot in my pistol, saw him fall from his saddle and dragged away rearward in the stirrups by his terrified horse. The act gave the others time to near me, and I must have perished within sight of the city but for a few cavalry who were sent out to succour me. I had been seen by Colonel Dennie of ours, who made that remark which is now historical.

' " Ackbar Khan has sworn that but one man shall escape alive, and, by heaven, yonder *he* comes !"

'In Jellalabad my wounds were dressed. I had food, succour, and rest for the body, but not of the mind, for almost the first tidings that Vassal Holland had for me concerned our lost ones. The ruffian Ackbar had despatched the hostages, as they were named—Lady Sale, Lady Macnaghten, and their fair companions—towards Toorkistan, to be there sold as slaves and bondwomen to the Usbec Tartars, greater savages, if possible, than the Afghans themselves.

' By this time the general was dead. He had expired in the tower of Zemaun Khan.

'I now remembered the words of Nourmahal, on that evening which proved so fatal to her, that "whether given as hostages in peace, or taken as spoil in war, the Feringhee women will become the gholaums—the slaves of the Afghan chiefs."

'"So they still live, Vassal?" said I, with a groan.

'"Yes; but for what a fate—for what a fate! I would rather hear that my poor Bella were dead!"

'Eight months passed after this—eight months of acute horror and terrible anxiety to all who had, as we had, a tender interest in the lost; and common humanity made all sympathise with such as Sir Robert Sale, who had a wife and daughter in such butcherly hands.

'How these months were passed, and all we did, if detailed, would far exceed the limits of my story; suffice it, that we joined the "Army of Vengeance," as it was named—the army that again marched, but in triumph, up those terrible passes which were literally paved with whitening human remains and the bones of horses and other baggage animals—the army which drove the Afghan tribes like chaff before the wind, fought victoriously the battle of Tizeen, and raised a shout of triumph when it came again in sight of Cabul, when the standard of Ackbar Khan was trod in the bloody dust, and the flames of ruin enveloped the great Balahissar.

'This was on the 12th of October, just about a year from that night when I had seen Mabel Berriedale, in all her girlish beauty, at Lady Sale's, and we had the unlucky adventure with the pocket-book. Ages seemed to have elapsed since then!

'"I have news for you, gentlemen," said the white-haired Sir Robert Sale (whose services dated back to the wars against Tippoo Sahib), as he came hurriedly one morning into the place which we had improvised as a mess-bungalow, in the now ruined cantonments— "most welcome news," he added emphatically, as his voice broke and tears filled his eyes, "and doubly so to a husband and father, like me. Thanks to the courage, diplomacy, and daring of Sir Richmond Shakespeare, at the head of 600 Kuzzilbash Lancers, the whole of the ladies have been rescued, when *en route* to Toorkistan, and are now on their way to join us here."

'He fairly broke down as he said this, and covered his face with his handkerchief. A half cheer rose from the group in the bungalow, where there was not an eye unmoistened. Then Sir Robert looked up and said:

'In a few minutes we shall march to meet them!

There go the bugles of ours! See," he added, with a sparkling eye, "how the 13th are rushing to the muster-place, actually belting themselves as they come along!"

'Under Sir Robert's orders, in less than an hour we had left Cabul behind us. With the 13th Light Infantry he had the 3rd Light Dragoons (now Hussars), the first Bengal Cavalry, and a train of mountain guns, to keep any wandering horde in awe.

'Light were the hearts of the soldiers as they marched along. Cheerfully had they ever marched—to battle and siege, at Ghuzni, Jellalabad, and Cabul, but more cheerfully did they now depart on their errand of mercy and succour; and they marched with a rapidity I have never seen equalled, save in the advance on Lucknow.

'Vassal Holland was more hopeful than I was. Dreadful doubts suggested themselves to me from time to time. I might hear that Mabel Berriedale had died months ago; that she might have been abducted for the rarity of her beauty, and that an impenetrable veil obscured her fate! Ackbar was said to have appropriated one of the captives. Heavens, if it proved to be Mabel!

'Her figure came before me as I saw it last—the

memory of her voice choked in tears, and the tremulous pressure of her hand, while the warning bugles
blew, and it was too late to speak—too late to
explain!

' Ere long a dark group appeared advancing, with
glittering spears, out of a valley, as Sale's command
attained the crest of a hill. It was Sir Richmond,
with the ladies and the Lancers!

' A shout burst from the soldiers, and actually
breaking their ranks, they rushed forward, and with
loud cheers greeted all, but chiefly Lady Sale and her
widowed daughter.

' In another moment I had both Mabel and Bella
in my arms, till Vassal drew the latter from me.
Many now met friends from whom they had long
been parted, as if in death. Wives threw themselves
into the arms of husbands, daughters embraced
fathers, and the artillery fired a salute that shook the
hills of Jubcais.

' " Papa—I do not see papa !" said Mabel anxiously.

' " Lay your head on my breast, darling, and I will
whisper all !"

' " He is dead, then ; and poor mamma too is gone !
I have no one in the world——"

' " But me, darling !" said I, as I kissed her tears
away and assisted her to remount.

'Here ends my story. We were to have been married when we returned to Old England had not events occurred which I cannot tell you now, but the results of which are swiftly passing away, and I shall be soon able to call her my own after long years of waiting, having had enough and to spare of Afghanistan and the Khyber Mountains.'

DICK STAPLES

OF

THE 'QUEEN'S OWN.'

DICK STAPLES OF THE 'QUEEN'S OWN.'

WHEN I came back, boys, after my fighting in India was over, you laughed at my old red coat (for I had no other)—a trifle tattered, I dare say it was, as well it might be, after all I had gone through in it latterly ; but you never forgot, boys, that it was the old Red Rag, that tells of England's glory !

The company to which I belonged—the Grenadiers of the 'Queen's Own' (for Grenadiers were not abolished till soon after the time of the Indian Mutiny)—was cantoned at Jubbulpore, in the month of July, when all Bengal was seething with revolt, and murder and outrage were occurring everywhere. All was quiet as yet in Jubbulpore, which I may tell you is in Berar, on the tableland of the Deccan ; but ugly rumours came from time to time about the 50th and 52nd Bengal Sepoy regiments, who were stationed at Nagode, the nearest post to us, and which, of all the Bengal army, were eventually the last to revolt.

Neither tongue nor pen can describe what we—the handful of Europeans among the millions of India—endured at that terrible time, when the souls of fathers and mothers, of husbands and wives, daily grew sick with anxiety, while the atrocities of Delhi and Cawnpore, and more than a hundred other places, made our soldiers go mad in their longing for revenge. But all that is history now.

In the same cantonments with us was a regiment of Punjaubees, who had as yet remained quiet; but more could not be said of them, and we of the Queen's Own watched them closely, for we were only one to ten of them, and as no order for disarming them had come, we pretended to trust them, and affected a frankness and faith in our bearing with them we were far from feeling.

Thus, cantonment life went on pretty much the same as usual—the parade after gunfire, the officers and ladies riding or driving on the course, or the former idling in the verandas of the bungalows, sipping iced drinks or brandy-pawnee, studying the last Bengal *Hurkaru* or the thermometer; and the pandies cooking their food—rice and chillies, chupatties and ghee, under the glaring sun, in their own lines, and careful that the baleful shadow of no European passer should, during the process, fall across it. Our chief fear was that the approach of some thousand natives and deserters, led by Koer Sing, steeped in slaughter and flushed with conquest and crime, might in an hour change the face of things, and find us fighting for bare existence with the very men who shared the garrison duty of the cantonment with us.

Captain Basil Heron, who commanded us—a handsome man, in the prime of life, a great favourite with us all, and the leader in all manly sports and schemes for our welfare—with Captain Dalton, who commanded the Punjaubees, began to take quietly some measures to render the Residency, the only brick edifice there, more defensible than it was, a place wherein to place the European women and children in case of emergency.

Captain Heron had a wife—a fair and delicate English girl—and one little child, on whom they both doted; and when I saw the expression of haggard anxiety their faces wore, and the faces of others who had such charges to love and protect, I thanked Heaven that then and there I had neither wife nor child to care for, nor aught to look after but my old 'Brown Bess.'

Rumours that precautions were being taken spread like lightning through the native lines, and Buktawur Sing, the Subadar-Major of the Punjaubees, a grotesquely ferocious-looking fellow, with a large hook nose, and black mustachios of such enormous length that they floated over his shoulders, went to Captain Heron, and, with his base eyes full of tears, besought him not to send the ladies and children out of the cantonments, as the whole of his regiment had sworn on the waters of the Ganges 'to be true to their salt.' Captain Heron heard this promise doubtfully ; but Mrs. Heron, who sat there with her baby crowing in her lap, its fat fingers clutching at the golden curls that clustered round her forehead, besought her husband to believe him.

But although he salaamed and bowed very low indeed, my particular chum and comrade, Bill Brierly, who had been more than twelve years in India, expressed to me his firm belief that this was all acting, and that 'the time was at hand when we might look out for squalls !'

And I was sure Bill was right, for I had been on duty as an orderly in the veranda on the evening when Buktawur Sing quitted the captain's bungalow, and there was no vestige of his crocodile's tears as he passed me ; but a broad grin spread over his brown face, and a cruel leer came into his eyes as he paused for a few seconds, and listened to the voice of Mrs. Heron, who was singing at the piano.

Despite the promises of Buktawur Sing, Captain Heron, as senior officer, posted a picquet at some distance from the cantonments on the road to Nagode, to cut off communication with the two regiments there—at least, to prevent any concerted movement being arranged.; and all postal matters being then at a standstill, we knew little about what was going on around us, but heard only vague and terrifying rumours.

On a night early in July, I was detailed for the picquet on the Nagode road, and Captain Heron resolved to accompany it, though it was under Mr. Drayton of Ours, a middle-sized and handsome fellow, with a delicate-looking face, and much of that self-esteem and imperturbable confidence of character peculiar to many young Englishmen. He had seen service, too, and had on his breast the Crimean medals.

As we paraded in front of Captain Heron's bungalow, he came forth with his sword and revolver, and his pretty young wife clinging to his arm.

'Are you compelled to go, Basil?' she asked.

'No; yet somehow I feel impelled to-night; but

retire, Rose. Good-night, dear—you look tired; to bed, and pleasant dreams to you.'

'You have your flask and the sandwiches, and your great-coat?'

'Everything. How thoughtful you are! Good-night, and kiss baby for me.'

We marched out through the lines; but Mrs. Heron, who had some sad foreboding, watched the picquet as long as it was in sight. Heron and Drayton chose their halting-place and threw out their advanced sentinels a considerable distance in front of the picquet. Of these, I was one, and my orders were, on the advance of any armed party, to fall back softly and silently, and communicate the alarm. Alone on my post there, keeping watch with the stars, and the whole sweep of country before me, memory went back to the old, or rather the young, days of my boyhood, even to yonder old mill, when I worked there; the rabbits in the brake, the squirrels in the trees, the nuts and berries in the hedgerows; till suddenly the galloping of a horse roused me, and I cocked my musket. The sound came from the front!

Another moment and the rider was before me, and reined up. He evidently had heard nothing of the picquet, and was enraged to find me barring the way.

By his uniform he was a subadar of the 50th B. N. Infantry, and mounted on an officer's horse.

'The parole?' said I.

'How should I know it? I have just come from Nagode,' said he, in broken English; adding, 'Stand back, Kafir!'

'Oh ho!' I exclaimed, as the epithet warned me at once of enmity; and grasping his reins, 'What news have you from that quarter?' I asked.

'Only that the faithful have risen at last, and not one of the accursed *Ghora Logue* (*i.e.*, white people) will be left alive—not even the youngling at its mother's breast, and all in Jubbulpore shall perish too!' he added through his clenched teeth, while his eyes blazed with fury, and he attempted to draw his sword; but ere he could do so, and as his horse rose on its haunches for an onward bound, I jerked the powerful curb with such violence to the rear, that ere the sword had left its scabbard, man and horse were prostrate on the road—the former stunned and senseless. In a moment more I was in his saddle and galloping back to report to Captain Heron all I had heard from the envoy of the mutineers.

The picquet had barely got under arms when a great hubbub was heard coming on from the front, but no appearance of armed men, though the moon had now shone forth. It was chiefly the rolling of wheels and clatter of hoofs, and ere long there came up a wild and terrified throng of European fugitives from Nagode—dishevelled women, exasperated men, and wailing children. In a word, on the approach of the rebels under Koer Sing, the 50th and 52nd had broken out into open mutiny; but, by some merciful interposition of Providence, had permitted their officers, with their families, to fly to Jubbulpore, where they hoped for a time, at least, to find protection and safety.

Captain Heron was in the act of promising both, when a cry escaped him, for a sound of scattered musket-shots was heard in our *rear*, and flames were shooting up from every quarter of the cantonments of Jubbulpore.

'The Punjaubees have revolted!' exclaimed everyone. The sentinels were called in, and the picquet fell back at 'the double'—every heart beating wildly. Upwards of thirty straw-roofed bungalows and innumerable haystacks were blazing at once, casting a lurid glare on the country for miles around; great pinnacles of wavering and many-coloured flames, with huge volumes of smoke, rose into the air of the sultry night, the roar of the conflagration mingling with the yells of the rioters and the shrieks of the perishing.

Under Buktawur Sing, whom some other messenger had reached, the Punjaubees had revolted, looted and destroyed the bungalows, and gone off to Nagode, killing every European who failed to reach the Residency, taking with them, 'as hostages,' Mrs. Heron, with her baby, and a Lieutenant Macgregor. Wild wrath swelled up in all our hearts, as we looked around us, and collected the dead—the gashed bodies of brave men, of helpless women and children ; and I shall never forget the face of Captain Heron, as he clung to Mr. Drayton's arm, and looked at the flaming bungalow to which he had brought his bride last year.

Henceforth,' said he, 'life will seem a blank behind me—worse than all, a blank before me, with a memory floating through it—the memory of her, and our poor little baby!' and he covered his face with his hands. 'My poor little wife! that I should have been so near, and yet utterly powerless to save her!'

'Hold up, bear up, for Heaven's sake, old fellow!' I heard Drayton say ; 'surely even these wretches will not have the heart to hurt a hair of her head.'

But Basil Heron answered only with a groan, yet not a tear escaped him. His grief and horror seemed too deep for even tears ; every man of the Queen's

Own there, felt that he could face death or anything to rescue her and make him happy ; but too probably only unavailing vengeance was left to us ! However, we had no time for much reflection. We took up our quarters in the Residency, all that were left of us, resolved, if attacked, to sell our lives as dearly as possible.

We entrenched and fortified it to the best of our means. The verandas were bricked up, leaving only loopholes to fire through. Sandbags were placed all round the roof, which was flat ; we staked the ground all about it to prevent a rushing attack, laid in grain for three months, and got two field-pieces planted in front of the house, to command the approach. We had in our care ten ladies, a number of sergeants and writers' wives, and ever so many children. In all we numbered now only about fifty fighting men, including officers, to furnish guards night and day, as we were in hourly expectation of an attack. Poor Captain Heron—the ghost of his former self—superintended all this, but day by day went past without tidings of his wife and child, and he would rather have known that they were lying, where so many others lay, in the burial-pit close by, in rest and peace, than endure the awful uncertainty that he did as to their fate.

After a time we heard that the rebels and mutineers

of that quarter were all massed, and living riotously, under the ex-Subadar-Major Buktawur Sing, in a place called Kuttingee, ten miles from Jubbulpore. They numbered several thousands—too strong for us to attack, and not even to save his wife dared Captain Heron risk the lives of his soldiers. And now it was that my comrade, Bill Brierly, came so manfully to the front. He was a queer fellow, Bill, and early in life had been—so the Queen's said—a strolling player. He was always merry and laughing, sang a good song, and was up to all kinds of larks; so now he volunteered to go to Kuttingee disguised as a *bud-mash*—one of the idle and rascally sort of irregular soldiers who loaf about bazaars, and are up to all kinds of mischief—and as such try to obtain some tidings of Mrs. Heron.

'Fifty guineas—aye, all I have in the world—are yours for any news you bring me, Brierly; even if they be evil,' said the captain, in a broken voice.

'Sir, I don't do this for money,' replied Bill; 'but for love of yourself and the poor young lady, who was so kind to me when in hospital—down with jungle fever. I risk my life daily for a shilling; why should not I do so, once at least, for her?'

'God bless you, Brierly!' said the captain, wringing his hand. 'God bless you!'

How I envied Bill, and would gladly have gone with him, but he—used to acting, knowing the lingo and the ways of the country, and how to comport himself—could alone perform the perilous task he undertook, knowing well, too, the while, that if he fell into the enemy's hands by being discovered, he would suffer a death as elaborately cruel as these barbarians could devise. He attired himself in a blue silk koortah, over a muslin shirt; a yellow-coloured chintz was wrapped round his shoulders; he wore a green turban and white cummerbund, or sash, in which he placed a brace of double-barrelled pistols carefully loaded. His face and neck to the shoulders and his hands to the wrists were coloured with lamp-black, the cork he used being dipped in oil to cause the colour to adhere; and thus disguised, he left the Residency, singing as he went—

> ' Sing hey, sing ho for the army O !
> Sing hey for the fame of the army O !
> A shilling a day is very fine pay,
> Then buckle and away for the army O !'

And we watched him, as, after the heat of mid-day was past, he took, alone, the road that led to Kuttingee.

Three days passed, and as there was no sign of poor

Bill coming back, we began to fear the worst—that 'the niggers' had discovered and cruelly killed him.

After perils or risks that might be spun out into a volume, Bill got past the outposts and sentries of the rebels and found himself in Kuttingee—ostensibly a *budmash*—willing to serve, for money or mischief, Buktawur Sing, or anyone else. Riot and disorder seemed to prevail in every quarter, though for their own safety the rebel Sepoys maintained a kind of discipline, and had guards and sentries posted. On all hands were seen the plunder of villas and bunga- lows. In the bazaar, three European heads were hung in a *bhoosa* bag, or forage-net, and Bill looked at them with anxiety lest one might prove the head of her he had come to seek tidings of.

Three days were passed without progress being made; but on the third he succeeded beyond his expectation.

When loitering near the gate of the fort, which overlooked the town of Kuttingee, he jostled unex- pectedly a Sepoy in the uniform of an officer, all save a huge green turban, who was about to enter the gate.

'*Chullo Sahib!*' (Come, sir!), the latter exclaimed angrily; 'what in the name of Jehannum are you about?'

Bill's heart leaped on finding himself face to face

with Buktawur Sing, the commander of all the rascal multitude in the place !

'Who are you ?' demanded the ex-Subadar-Major.

'Sookham Lall, a budmash, in want of a captain.'

'From whence ?'

'Jubbulpore, last.'

'Jubbulpore ! What are the cursed Kafirs doing there ?'

Bill described in somewhat exaggerated terms the fortification and garrison of the Residency.

'We may bring guns against it,' said Buktawur.

'They too have got guns,' replied Bill, though he knew that the Residency could no more stand a bombardment than a house of cards.

'And now, what do you want here ?' asked Buktawur, his black beady eyes gleaming suspiciously.

'To kill your Christian prisoners, just to keep my hand in,' replied Bill, grinding his teeth ; 'you have twenty, I understand.'

'I have only two here—the Sahib Macgregor and the Mehm Sahib Heron (her brat is not worth counting) ; there they are in the garden.'

Bill laid a hand on his tulwar.

'Not so fast, my friend,' said Buktawur, with a grin, 'for she is to be my wife ; and if matters go hard with me I may want the Sahib's head.'

'So they live yet!' thought Bill, as he entered the garden of the fort, but dared not approach them, though looking sharply at them, and viewing the strong defences of the place, and the avenues that led to it.

In a kind of alcove, excavated out of the solid rock of the fort, Mrs. Heron—clad now partly like a native woman—was seated with her baby in her lap, and near her Lieutenant Macgregor, as if for companionship or the sympathy he dared scarcely to manifest. He was in the rags of his uniform, and both looked haggard and wasted with the anxieties and troubles they had undergone.

Bill drew near her, but at that moment a Sepoy came to Buktawur for orders.

'Don't start, Mrs. Heron,' he whispered, 'or seem to see or hear me—I'm Billy Brierly, of your husband's company. He is well and unwounded, and counts every hour till he can rescue you.'

Bill then drew back, for now Buktawur Sing came hastily and suspiciously forward. Mrs. Heron looked up. Astonishment, gratitude and hope were expressed in her eyes by tears, but not a ray of joy shone in them; and honest Bill Brierly felt his heart wrung as he looked on the poor lady, and saw now that the baby she held in her lap was dead!

He mentioned this to Buktawur Sing.

'*Kootch purwanni*' ('Never mind'), replied the latter, laughing to see her bending over it in the depth of her misery, and playing with his little white hands and flaxen curls.

'My little Basil—my little Basil!' she kept repeating; 'my little sunbeam gone! But safe now—safe from peril and suffering—safe with the Good Shepherd. And I am here!'

As if to show his weariness or contempt of this, the ferocious Buktawur Sing snatched the child from her, and, with an imprecation, cast it into the alligator tank in the centre of the garden. She uttered a wild shriek and fell forward on her face senseless. Macgregor started to her assistance, but was driven back by the sharp bayonet of a Sepoy sentry; and Brierly, finding that he was powerless to give any aid whatever, quitted the place, and with a sob for vengeance in his throat, took the way back to Jubbulpore.

Bill mercifully remained silent as to the fate of the child; but poor young Captain Heron was never weary of questioning him as to it and the unhappy mother.

'It is a sore trial to me, Brierly,' said he, in a broken voice.

'Yes, sir,' he replied ; 'but He who sends the trial sends the strength to bear it too.'

'Bear it like a man,' urged Drayton.

'But I must also *feel* it as a man,' replied poor Heron, unconsciously quoting the words of Macduff.

And now came tidings that filled us all with grim and stern joy. The movable column of the Madras troops, under General Miller, was on the march from Dumoh to attack the rebels in Kuttingee, and drawing out from the Residency every man fit for service, Captain Heron set off to join him ; and I can remember how, on the march, he kept near the section where Brierly was, for the latter had seen and spoken with the creature *he* loved most on earth. A ghastly and haggard man Heron looked now—the shadow of his former self.

Though it was only a ten-miles tramp, and, leaving knapsacks behind, we had only our great-coats and blankets to carry, I shall never forget that day's march to Kuttingee ! It was one of thirst and toil, with all our canteens and water-bottles empty. We pushed on under a noonday sun, under which the parched earth seemed to pant like a living creature. The streams were dried up, and all that was green had become yellow and sickly in hue ; the sky seemed a furnace—the sun a globe of fire. Clouds of dust surrounded our line of march, and sand-spouts rose at times; the ravens and kites gaped with wide-open beaks by the wayside, and the alligators lay hidden to the muzzle in their oozy tanks. Fissures gaped in the soil; the birds were hushed, and insect-life stood still; the 'burra choop,' or Great Silence, as the Hindoos call it, reigned around us, and we had three cases of sunstroke; yet we pushed manfully on, and when evening drew near found ourselves in front of Kuttingee.

The first shot might be the death-knell of Mrs. Heron and all other Christian prisoners, so the emotions with which her husband surveyed it as he marched the remains of his company into the assigned position may be imagined.

The outworks of the fort were armed with cannon, which opened on our columns as soon as they were within range, and to which ours were not slow in replying, and making a considerable slaughter of the infantry that lined the summit of the walls and towers, which their return fire seemed to garland with flashes and smoke. We of the Queen's, as a flank company, had the Minié rifle (which by force of habit we still called Brown Bess), and in closing up we took cover under every bush or stone, and picked off the rebels by steady pot-shots delivered from the knee. We carried the outworks by a furious rush at the point of the bayonet, and then slewed round a couple of the heaviest guns, by which we blew in the gate of the keep, or central fort. Beyond was a traverse, over which the rebels were firing; a tempest of balls swept through the arch as the wind sweeps a tunnel, and there fell many of ours, and among them poor Bill Brierly.

Our loud hurrahs replied to the yells of ' Deen-deen !' (' Faith !') and ' Death to the Kafirs, the Fering-hees, the Ghora Logue !' while maddened by bhang, opium and churuis, the infuriated Sepoys met us hand to hand, but only to go down on every side ; for, with our bugles sounding the ' advance,' we stormed the traverse at a rush, and spread all over the garden within the square fort.

We fought our way desperately. ' Remember the ladies—remember the babies !' were our cries. Near the alligator tank lay the bodies of a European man and woman. They were those of Lieutenant Mac-gregor and Mrs. Heron, before whom he had thrown himself twice, as she was cut down by the tulwar of Buktawur Sing, and the blood was yet flowing from her wound when we found her. As for the poor officer, he was found, as the General reported, ' with a hole through the neck, both arms broken, and his body perforated by upwards of thirty wounds.'

I was an old soldier even then. I had been in many battles, and seen much of death and suffering, but I felt a choking in my throat as I saw Basil Heron, kneeling, sword in hand, by the side of his wife for a moment, ere he rushed away, intent on revenge.

Hemmed in a corner, amid a heap of dead and dying, he ere long found Buktawur Sing, and, though I did not see it, close and terrible was the combat that ensued between them.

'At last! at last I have him! God, I thank Thee!' he exclaimed, with a fervour that mingled with just indignation; and he ordered Drayton to stand back, and the soldiers, who were ready to shoot the reptile down, to leave him to his own fate. Buktawur was armed with a ponderous tulwar, edged like a razor; and Heron, fortunately for himself, had not one of our regulation tailors' swords, but a straight good-cutting blade that his father had used in Central India. His teeth were set; he panted rather than breathed; his cheek was pale—his eyes were blazing, and sparks of fire flew from their swords at every stroke. But fate was against Buktawur Sing; he received in his body a succession of cuts and thrusts that brought him, with blood flowing from every vein, upon his knees, and when his turban fell off, by one trenchant slash Basil Heron clove him from the brain to the chin, and with his foot fiercely he spurned the corpse as it sunk before him.

    *   *   *   *   *   *

' Where is she ?' he gasped hoarsely of me and others, as he staggered back to the side of the alligator tank, and found that his wife had disappeared.

' Inside the fort. Calm yourself. We have laid her on a charpoy, poor girl !' said Drayton.

' My poor Rose! my poor Rose!' moaned Heron, as he covered his face, and the hot tears streamed through his fingers. Through a place where 150 of the 52nd alone were lying dead, he was led into a darkened room, where, after the roar of the storm and capture, all seemed dreadfully still. On a charpoy, or native bed, lay Rose Heron, and Sheikh Abdul Ali, a native doctor, was bathing and binding up the wound ; and, nerving himself for what he had to look upon, her husband drew near, and with trembling hands drew back the mosquito-curtains.

Was he dreaming ? was it a mockery or a delusion that he saw Rose there—not dead—not even dying ; but with her eyes seeking for him—blood already mantling in her pale cheek ? And he learned that the blow of the felon's tulwar had—though cutting her tender forehead—only stunned her, for the hand of Macgregor had caused the blade to turn in his grasp!

Some bright beams often fall from the gloomiest sky. So husband and wife had met again, and—after all they had undergone—survived to spend the coming Christmas at home in old England, and to hear the merry chimes in their peaceful Kentish village ring out upon the frosty air the message of Peace and Goodwill to All.

THE STORY

OF

LIEUTENANT JAMES MOODY

OF

BARTON'S REGIMENT.

THE STORY

OF

LIEUTENANT JAMES MOODY

OF

BARTON'S REGIMENT.

THE exploits of this adventurous but forgotten Scot, who nearly perished miserably on an American scaffold, like Major André of the Cameronians, surpassed in some respects even those of Captain Colquhoun Grant, the famous scouting officer of Wellington, so extolled by Napier in his 'History of the Peninsular War.'

During the progress of the strife with our revolted colonists in America, he rendered himself famous by the skill and audacity with which he intercepted many of their mails and brought them into New York, then the British headquarters after the Battle of Long Island. In May, 1780, when an ensign, with four trusty soldiers he penetrated into New Jersey, for the purpose of surprising Governor Livingstone, who cruelly oppressed the royalists, but failing to achieve his capture, his next idea was to blow up the maga-zine at Suckasanna, which also proved abortive, as he found it guarded by above one hundred bayonets. On being joined by a few soldiers who had been taken with Burgoyne at Saratoga, he entered the mountain-ous county of Sussex, in the principal gaol of which, he learned, several prisoners were confined for their loyalty, and among them a poor soldier of Burgoyne's, who had been doomed to death ; merely for being a royalist. Moody determined on achieving the release of this man and all the other prisoners.

Selecting six men he came to the gaol door late at night, and his business was demanded by the keeper from an open window.

'I have here a prisoner to put into your custody,' he replied.

'Is he one of Moody's fellows?' asked the gaoler, at a venture.

'Yes, exactly so,' replied the ensign, giving the name of some noted Tory in the neighbourhood, and desiring the keeper to come for him.

The latter declined, saying that 'Moody was about, and he had orders to admit no man after sunset.'

'I am Ensign Moody,' said that officer sternly; 'I have a strong party with me, and if you do not surrender your keys, I will blow the place about your ears!'

His men now imitated the Indian war-whoop, and shouted, 'The Indians—the Indians have come!'

On this the gaoler, his assistants, and even many of the townspeople, fled to the woods. Moody then burst into the gaol through the window, and found the condemned soldier in his cell fast asleep.

'There is no possibility,' says Moody's Narrative (now out of print), 'of describing the agony of this man when he saw before him a man in arms, attended by persons he was utterly at a loss to recognise. The first and only idea that occurred to him was, that, as many of the friends of the government had been privately executed in prison, the person he saw was his executioner!'

Moody released and carried off with him all the prisoners, including the soldier, who, by a strange freak of fortune, was afterwards taken again during the war, and hanged in the same prison, and in virtue of the old sentence, though we are told that his only crime was 'an unshaken allegiance to his sovereign.' This seems barely probable, as another soldier, a Scotsman named Robert Maxwell, was executed at the same time for robbery and plunder.

On the 6th of March, 1781, when Moody was still an ensign, the Adjutant-General, Oliver de Lancy, of the 17th Light Dragoons, successor in office to the ill-fated André, proposed ' an expedition into the rebel country, for the purpose of intercepting the despatches of Mr. Washington.' Moody instantly undertook the task, and marching his party twenty-five miles that night, concealed them in a morass; but the guide lost heart, which so enraged Moody that he would have shot him, but for the sake of his wife and family, and was compelled to return to New York. Colonel de Lancy was much disappointed; the guide was made a prisoner, and on the 11th of the same month Moody set forth again, and reached the Haverstraw Mountains, which overlook the Hudson, amid a snow-storm, and by the 15th he captured the despatches and their bearer; but so great were the hardships undergone that some of his men perished of cold and hunger. For this, Moody, who had been one year a volunteer, and three an ensign, was promoted to a lieutenancy.

About the middle of May the adjutant-general, being in want of intelligence, suggested to Moody the capture of another 'rebel mail;' and on the night of the 15th he set forth with four well-armed men, and after proceeding many miles, he found himself beset on three sides by a considerable number of the

Colonial troops, who, having secret intelligence of his movements from New York, were then in ambush awaiting him.

On the fourth side lay a ridge of cliffs, so steep and rugged that to escape by it seemed impossible. There was no alternative now but to surrender and die, or leap down the cliffs, and in the dark. Calling on his men to follow him, the daring Moody sprang down, and as the soil was soft at the base, they were all unhurt, though seriously shaken. They now crossed a swamp, only to find themselves before a still stronger party of the enemy when day was breaking. To advance was impossible, as there was no doubt that they had been betrayed. They contrived to creep away unseen, and travelled till they gained the North River within four miles of New York. Just when Moody conceived they were out of all peril, a party of seventy men, under arms, issued from a wayside house, and opened fire upon him. 'He received one general discharge, and thought it a miracle he escaped unwounded ; the bullets fell like a storm of hail around him ; his clothes were shot through in several places ; one ball pierced his hat, another grazed his arm. Without at all slackening his pace, he turned round, discharged his musket, and killed one of his pursuers ; still they kept up their fire, each man discharging his piece as fast as he could load ; but gaining an opportunity of soon doubling upon them, he gave them the slip, and in due time arrived once more safe in New York.'*

He departed again on the same perilous errand for Pompton, on the 18th May, conceiving that the foe would think they had sufficiently scared him from further expeditions of the kind. With four resolute fellows, he crossed the Hakinsack river by a canoe which he concealed among the long, rank sedges, and soon fell in with an American patrol, whose object was to prevent the conveyance of provisions to the British headquarters. He was ordered to stand or be instantly shot. With his four men, he fired, and then gave an order as if he had a strong force in reserve, on which the patrol fled.

A four miles' march brought them to the Saddle river, which had overflown its banks; the night was gloomy and tempestuous, and a body of American regulars held the bridge. He was thus compelled to ford the river, a task of great danger and difficulty. Rumour said that 'Moody was out,' and the mail instead of being sent as usual, by the way of Pompton, was sent by another way under a guard. Selecting a man whose voice, face, and tall figure resembled his own,

* ' Political Magazine," vol. iv.

he sent him to a certain justice of the peace in another neighbourhood, who at once fled to the woods, giving out everywhere that Moody was *there*. To that quarter the Colonial troops were at once despatched, while Moody captured the mail at another, and brought in all the despatches relative to the important interview between General Washington and Count Rochambeau in Connecticut. After this, Moody captured two more bags of despatches, in one expedition being aided by his younger brother, who must have been a mere lad, as he himself was then only in his twenty-fourth year.

In October, 1781, Captain and Brevet-Major George Beckwith, of the 37th Regiment, then aide-de-camp to Lieutenant-General Baron Knyphausen, informed Mr. Moody that a person named Addison had suggested a project of great moment—to bring off all the books and papers of the Congress! This Englishman had held some inferior office under Thompson, the Secretary to the Congress, and, being a prisoner of war, it was resolved that he should be released, return to his old employment at Philadelphia, where Moody would visit him—Major Beckwith vouching for his fidelity.

Moody undertook this perilous duty with the full knowledge that Addison might deem *him* well worth betrayal; thus he stipulated that the former was to be kept in ignorance that he had undertaken it. Moody took with him only his brother John and another Scotsman, named Marr, on whom he could rely, and a night—the 2nd of November—and place were appointed where they were to meet the traitor Addison, in the vicinity of Philadelphia.

They met him duly, but Lieutenant Moody kept a little in the background lest his figure, which was a tall one, might be recognised by Addison, who was at once accosted by his brother and Marr. The former told them that everything was ready; that he had obtained access to the most secret archives of the Senate House, and that next evening he would deliver up all the books and papers they were in quest of. Mutual assurances of fidelity were exchanged. They crossed the river together in a boat for Philadelphia, unaccompanied by Moody, whose first foreboding or suspicion was a right one, for the perfidious Addison had already sold him and his companions to the Congress!

Pretending that the precise time at which their plans could be executed was dubious, Addison suggested that Lieutenant Moody should remain at the ferryhouse opposite the city till they returned; and before departing he told a keeper of it that the

visitor was an officer of the New Jersey Brigade,
which the woman understood to be the force of that
name under Washington. To avoid notice, Moody
affected indisposition, and remained in a room up-
stairs, but with his arms ready, awake and on the
watch.

Next morning he overheard a man saying to
another :

'There is the very devil to pay in Philadelphia !
There has been a plot to break into the Senate
House, but one fellow has betrayed two who are now
taken, and a party of soldiers are coming to seize a
third, who is concealed somewhere hereabouts.'

On hearing this alarming intelligence, Moody took
his pistols, rushed downstairs, and escaped. He was
not one hundred yards from the house when he saw
the soldiers enter it ! He attempted to gain shelter
in a thicket by leaping a fence, but found the latter
lined by cavalry, and got concealment in a ditch,
under the overhanging weeds and shrubs. There he
lay for some time with pistols cocked, and heard the
soldiers pass and repass within ten yards of him.
From the ditch they went all round an adjacent field,
where he could see them probing the stacks of Indian
corn with their bayonets ; and conceiving rightly that
they would not explore there again, when night fell

he sought shelter in one; and as his pursuers were still about, he remained in an upright position in the stack, without food or drink, for two days and nights, enduring excruciating torture. The stacks were destitute of corn, being merely straw.

After a time he ventured, in the dark, to the bank of the Delaware, and finding a small boat, while full of grief for the peril of his brother and friend, pushed off and rowed up the river; and though many times accosted by people on the water, he replied to them 'in the rough phraseology of the gentlemen of the oar;' and escaping unsuspected, after many adventures and circuitous marches, all undergone in the night, in five days from the time of his landing, he reached in safety the British headquarters at New York. There was not the slightest hope that his brother would be pardoned, for the treason of Arnold and many recent events had infused much rancour in the minds of the contending parties. Tried by court-martial, the two prisoners were sentenced to death and executed. John Moody was in his twenty-third year, and on learning his fate, his father—an old and deserving soldier—lost his reason. The American bulletin runs thus in the papers of the time:

PHILADELPHIA, *November* 14, 1781.

'On Thursday morning last, Lawrence Marr and John Moody, of Colonel Barton's Tory Regiment, were apprehended on suspicion of being spies. On the following day they were indulged with a candid hearing before a board of officers, whereof the Hon. Major-General the Marquis de la Fayette was president. It appears that their business was to steal and carry off the Secret Journals of Congress to New York. . . . The Board having reported to the Hon. Board of War, their opinion was approved, and Marr and Moody were both sentenced to die, which sentence was executed on Moody between the hours of eleven and twelve; Marr is respited until the 23rd instant. . . . The enemy, who at this period seem equal to no exploits superior to robbing mails and stealing papers, may thank their beloved friend Benedict Arnold for the untimely death of the young man, who was only in his twenty-third year.'

Of the future career of the adventurous James Moody we unfortunately know nothing.

'OLD MINORCA;'

OR,

GENERAL MURRAY OF THE SCOTS FUSILIERS.

'OLD MINORCA;'

OR,

GENERAL MURRAY OF THE SCOTS FUSILIERS.

IT is strange that the life of this old officer has found no place in any biographical work; yet he was the successor of Wolfe at Quebec, and as such completed the conquest of Canada. He defended Minorca, and repelled with scorn De Crillon's offer of a million sterling to betray that post; and who, when an old lieutenant-general, was arraigned before a court-martial by the brilliant Sir William Draper, whom he signally baffled.

James Murray was the fifth son of Alexander, fourth Lord Elibank, who in 1698 married Elizabeth Stirling, daughter of a surgeon in Edinburgh. Following the example of his elder brother Patrick, who served as a colonel in the Carthagena Expedition under Lord Cathcart, he betook him to a military life, and on the 5th January, 1750-51, was lieutenant-colonel of the 15th Foot, then on the Irish Establishment (Millans' Lists). During five years subsequently his regiment was still serving in Ireland, and in 1757 he commanded in Sir John Mordaunt's expedition to Rochefort. On this service ten battalions of infantry sailed from the Isle of Wight on board eighteen ships of the line, attended by frigates, fire-ships, and bombketches, under Sir Edward Hawke and Admiral Knowles, on the 8th September, 'attended,' says Smollett, 'with the prayers of every man warmed with the love of his country and solicitous for her honour;' but, like most of those buccaneering expeditions to the coast of France which disgraced the reigns of the two first Georges, it proved a failure.

The fortifications of Aix, an island at the mouth of the Charente, and midway between Oleron and the mainland, were cannonaded, blown up, and demolished, at the cost of a million of money ; 'after which,' says Smollett, 'the officers, in a council of war, took the final resolution of returning to England, choosing rather to oppose the frowns of an angry sovereign, the murmurs of an incensed nation, and the contempt of mankind, than fight a handful of dastardly militia.'

Charged with disobedience of orders and instructions, Sir John Mordaunt was arraigned at Whitehall before a court-martial, which sat for six days, from the 14th to the 20th December, 1758. Among the members were Lord Tyrawly, Brigadier Huske (who was engaged at Falkirk), and Colonel William Kingsley, of Minden fame, the ancestor of the author of 'Alton Locke.' Wolfe was a witness for the prosecution, as was also 'Mr. Secretary William Pitt ;' and among those for the prisoner was Colonel Murray of the 15th, Cornwallis, and the two admirals. By the court Mordaunt was unanimously acquitted.

We next find James Murray at the capture of Louisbourg, in 1758. ('Records 21st Foot.')

Here the attacking force consisted of fourteen battalions of infantry, with 600 provincials, and 300 artillery—13,094 men in all, under Major-General Amherst. The place was taken by capitulation, when the garrison, which consisted of 5,637 men (including the battalions of Volontaires Etrangers, Cambize, Artois, and Burgundy), under the Chevalier de Dracour, laid down their arms.

On the 24th of October, 1759, James Murray was made Colonel Commandant of the 60th, or Royal Americans, and at the capture of Quebec he served as brigadier in command of the left wing ; and after the fall of Wolfe and surrender of the city—the fortifications of which were in tolerable order, though the houses were completely demolished—he was left with a garrison of 5,000 men to defend it ; while the rest of the forces returned to Britain with the fleet, which sailed soon, lest it should be locked up by ice in the River St. Lawrence. ('Ramsay's Military Memoirs.')

In the spring of 1760, Monsieur de Levi, at the head of 13,000 men, took the field and appeared on the Heights of Abraham, above Quebec, when Murray, who had lost 1,000 men by scurvy, had but two courses open to him—to march out and fight the enemy on the old battle-ground, where the grave of Montcalm still lay, or stand a siege within the ruins of the city. He chose the former, with equal spirit and resolution, and coming out, with only 3,000 effective men and twenty guns (says the 'Military Guide,' 1781), having to leave the rest of his force to overawe the inhabitants.

His daring struck the enemy with surprise, when he came in sight of them on the 28th of April, so vast was the disparity in force ! He found their first column advantageously posted on high ground covered with trees, and their main body in line in its rear. He attacked the first column with such fury and intrepidity that it was hurled in disorder on the second which, however, stood firm, and received him with a fire so close and well directed that his troops staggered under it. The strength and weight of the French force were such that his flank and even his rear were menaced, and after an obstinate struggle, with the loss of 1,000 of all ranks, he was compelled to fall back, but in good order, behind the walls of Quebec.

Undismayed, the ardour of his troops, who had only salt rations to live upon, redoubled ; and though the French began to invest the city in regular form on the very evening of their victory, it was the 11th of May before their guns opened. Murray had on the walls 132 pieces of cannon, many of which he was unable to handle for want of men ; and with all his bravery he must have been compelled to surrender, had not the arrival of Lord Colville's squadron in the St. Lawrence on the 15th, and the destruction of the French fleet there by some of his advanced frigates, so disheartened De Levi that he retired with precipitation, abandoning all his provisions, stores, and artillery, of which Murray instantly possessed himself.

Montreal was the only place of any consequence now held by France in Canada. There General the Marquis de Vaudrieul, governor of the province, commanded all that remained of the French army ; and as a portion of General Amherst's plan for its reduction, Colonel Haviland, of the 45th Regiment, with the troops under his command, took possession of an island in Lake Champlain, while General Murray, at the head of all that could be spared from Quebec, came by water to Montreal, which was attacked by 10,000 men, and capitulated in September, 1760, after which the French lost all footing in America, the operations in which were confined to Colonel Grant's expedition against the Cherokees.

On the 10th July, 1762, Murray was gazetted major-general, and in the following year was made Governor of Canada, the conquest of which he completed and brought steadily under British sway. He was made a lieutenant-general in May, 1772, in which year we find him Governor of Minorca, with a salary of £730, and Sir William Draper, K.B., Lieutenant-Governor, with the same allowance. On the 19th February, 1783, he was made full general.

The British Government, anxious to have a naval station further up the Mediterranean than Gibraltar, took possession of Minorca in 1708, and it was confirmed to them by the Treaty of Utrecht, and remained in possession of Britain till 1758, when it was taken by a French fleet and army, after the failure of an attempt to relieve it, which led to the tragic death

of the unfortunate Admiral Byng. At the peace of
1763 Minorca was restored to Britain, but in 1782 it
was retaken by the Spaniards, after a defence by
General Murray which was deemed one of the most
brilliant military events of the age.

Long and narrow, it is thirty-two miles by eight
in extent, with Mount Toro in its centre, nearly
5,000 feet in height, and has two of the finest harbours
in the world, Fornella and Port Mahon, the latter of
which is defended by Fort St. Philip, on a rocky
promontory of difficult access from the land side.

Murray's garrison in Fort St. Philip consisted of
only 2,692 men, of which number, including the
51st Foot (under Colonel Pringle), only 2,016 were
regulars, 200 seamen of the *Minorca* sloop-of-war;
and 400 of these were invalids—'worn-out soldiers,'
as he states, sent from Britain in 1775, and all were
more or less unhealthy. 'The officers of the four
regular regiments,' says General Murray, in his defence of himself, 'were in much better health than
the privates. This is easily accounted for, for all of
them (viz., the British), for *eleven* years, lived on *salt*
provisions. The quantity of vegetables they con-
sumed and the wine they drank, though it prevented
the immediate efforts of scurvy, could not hinder it
from tainting the blood. The officers had, until we

were invested, lived entirely on fresh provisions, and even after, that we were confined to the Fort, had wine and other refreshments bought at their own expense. They likewise passed the day in the Castle Square, and were only at night confined in the damp air of the *souterreins;* but even the officers, with all these advantages, began to be infected.' (*Political Magazine*, 1783.)

On Minorca being menaced by a siege, Murray sent his wife and family to Leghorn, and, preparing for a vigorous defence, shut himself up in Fort St. Philip, for hostilities had now begun with Spain (*Scottish Register*, 1794). He scuttled and sank the *Minorca* sloop-of-war at the entrance of the harbour, to prevent the approach of the enemy's ships, and on the 20th of August found himself blocked up by a French and Spanish army, which landed in Minorca without opposition, to the number of 16,000 men, under the Duc de Crillon, who took his title from a village of that name in the Department of Vaucluse, and who subsequently distinguished himself at the great siege of Gibraltar. He was afterwards joined by six French battalions from Toulon, under the Count de Falkenhagen.

So resolute was the defence made by General Murray, that the Duc de Crillon soon began to de-

spair of reducing the place, even with the vast forces
he had opposed to it, and secretly offered him (doubtless by order of the King of France) the immense
bribe of one million sterling for the surrender of the
fortress. Indignant at such an insult, he addressed
the following reply to the French commander:

'FORT ST. PHILIP, *October* 16, 1781.

'When your brave ancestor, so celebrated in the
"Memoires" of Sully, was desired by his sovereign to
assassinate the Duc de Guise, he returned the answer
that you should have done when you were charged to
assassinate the character of a man whose birth is as
illustrious as your own, or that of the Duc de Guise.
I can have no further communication with you, but in
arms. If you have any humanity, pray send clothing
for your unfortunate prisoners in my possession ; leave
it at a distance to be taken for them, because I will
admit of no contact for the future, but such as is
hostile to the most inveterate degree.'

Your letter,' replied the Duke, 'restores each of us
to our place ; it confirms me in the high opinion I
always had of you, and I accept your last proposal
with pleasure.'

As ammunition was becoming scarce, on the 15th

of the same month the general issued an order that cannon were not to be fired at single men, for the younger officers of the garrison, becoming weary of confinement, were wont to turn their guns 'at Bagats, or figures dressed like men, which the enemy exhibited in ridicule of our ineffectual firing,' and, curiously enough, this order was one of the chief charges brought against him, by Sir William Draper, at a subsequent time.

By the 5th of February Murray's garrison, by the ravages of inveterate scurvy, was so reduced, that only 660 men were fit for duty, and out of these 560 were tainted with the disease. 'No words,' says Captain Schomberg, in his 'Naval Chronology,' 'can paint the heroic valour and resolution of the brave troops of this garrison, which had to capitulate.

'Such was the uncommon spirit of the King's soldiers' (to quote the Hon. James Murray's despatch), 'that they concealed their disorders and inability, rather than go into hospital ; several men died on guard, after having stood sentry, their fate not being discovered till called upon for the relief, when it became their turn to mount again. Perhaps a more noble or more tragical scene was never exhibited, than the march of the garrison of St. Philip through the Spanish and French armies. It consisted of no more than 600 old and decrepit soldiers, 200 seamen, 120 of the Royal Artillery, 20 Corsicans, and 25 Greeks, Turks, Moors, and Jews. The two armies were drawn up in two lines, forming a way for us to march through; they consisted of 14,000 men, and reached from the glacis to George Town, where our battalion laid down their arms, declaring that they had surrendered to GOD ALONE, having the satisfaction to know that the victors could not plume themselves on taking a *hospital.* Such were the distressing figures of our men, that many of the Spanish and French troops are said to have shed tears as they passed them.'

His casualties were 108.

The Lieutenant-Governor of Minorca, Sir William Draper, K.C.B., a famous officer in those days, the conqueror of Manilla (who erected on Clifton Downs a beautiful cenotaph to the memory of the Old English 79th Foot, disbanded in 1763), thought proper, on the return of the garrison to Britain, to accuse General Murray of bad conduct during the siege, of profusion and waste of money and stores, of extortion, rapacity and cruelty. On these startling charges, the general was brought before a court-martial at the Horse Guards, in November, 1782, the proceedings of which were taken in shorthand by Mr. Gurney. The President was Sir George Howard, K.B., and among the members was Lieutenant-General Cyrus Trapaud, familiarly known as 'Old Trap,' the friend of Wolfe. 'In our attendance on this court-martial,' says a print of the time, 'it struck us as an uncommon circumstance, that although it was composed of very old officers, and of long service, yet all appeared hale, vigorous, and remarkably stout men, literally, to all appearance, fit to carry a musket.   . General Murray appeared much broke, but had the remains of a very stout man , he looked the old soldier! Sir William Draper looked exceedingly well, and in the flower of his age. His star was very conspicuous, and his left arm always so carefully disposed as never to eclipse it.'

General Murray was fully and honourably acquitted of all the charges, save two that were trivial, and for which he was sentenced to be reprimanded, though he urged that his 'age and broken constitution, worn out in the defence of Fort St. Philip,' were such that he probably could serve his country no more. On the finding of the Court being communicated to the King by the Judge Advocate, Sir Charles

Gould, he approved of 'the zeal, courage, and firmness with which General Murray had conducted himself in the defence of Fort St. Philip, as well as his former long and approved services,' and the reprimand was dispensed with. His Majesty further expressed his concern that such an officer as Sir William Draper should have suffered his judgment to have become so perverted as to bring such charges against a superior officer. The Court, apprehensive, from some intemperate expressions made use of by the former to the latter in a document, that the veterans would resort to their pistols, prescribed a form of apology to be made use of by Sir William, and to be acquiesced in by General Murray; but this affair, which in its day made much noise in the military world and in London society, did not quite end here, as the general was afterwards prosecuted by his countryman, Mr. Sutherland, Judge Advocate of Minorca, for suspending him in his office, and £5,000 damages were awarded him— a sum for which he was reimbursed by the House of Commons.

On the 5th June, 1789, he was made colonel of 21st Royal Scots Fusiliers; and died on the 18th of June, 1794, at Beaufort House, near Bath, in Sussex, the seat of Sir James B. Burgess, Bart., Commissioner of

Excise in Scotland. In military circles he was long remembered as ' Old Minorca.'

He left an MS. diary of his defence of Quebec, which was in possession of Mr. Robert Blackwood, publisher, of Edinburgh, in 1849, but appears never to have been printed.

THE END.

www.ingramcontent.com/pod-product-compliance
Lightning Source LLC
Chambersburg PA
CBHW060554030726
47498CB00005B/1379